GRAYLING'S SONG

KAREN CUSHMAN

GRAYLING'S
SONG

CLARION BOOKS   HOUGHTON MIFFLIN HARCOURT
BOSTON   NEW YORK

Clarion Books

3 Park Avenue

New York, New York 10016

Copyright © 2016 by Karen Cushman

Clarion Books is an imprint of
Houghton Mifflin Harcourt Publishing Company.

www.hmhco.com

The text was set in 13 pt. Centaur MT Std.

Hand-lettering by Leah Palmer Preiss

Library of Congress Cataloging-in-Publication Data is available.

ISBN 978-0-544-30180-1

Manufactured in the United States of America

DOC 10 9 8 7 6 5 4 3 2 1

4500590237

For the greathearted young woman
who is my own daughter, Leah,
and for Robbie Cranch,
the closest to a hedge witch that
the twenty-first century has.

It is not down in any map;
true places never are.

—Herman Melville, *Moby-Dick*

GRAYLING'S SONG

I

he mist hung low in the valley between the forest and the town. It dangled from tree branches like stockings on a washing line and curled around Grayling's head as she weeded and hoed and raked, readying the herb garden for its winter rest. When her basket was filled — angelica and agrimony, rosemary and the remains of the dill — she put her shoes on again, for she had been gathering the last of the summer herbs with her feet bare, as was proper. She stood still for a moment, letting mist settle on her shoulders like a damp cloak, and listened to the quiet.

Finally, picking up the basket, she headed home. The steeply roofed cottage of wattle and yellow-tinted daub sat in a bit of a clearing, shaded by an ancient apple tree. Its round-topped door of rowan wood was crisscrossed by iron bands against the evil designs of demons, ghosts, and ill-wishers of all sorts. Brass bells hung from the eaves, a swag of hazel rods and garlic festooned the little window, and smoke poured from the smoke hole in the roof. Grayling smiled to see it, as she always did. Despite her mother's endless tasks, the cottage meant comfort, safety, seclusion.

The day was mild enough for them to have the window open. Grayling could hear her mother singing while she crushed dried wormwood and nettle for a healing ointment. Her mother, Hannah Strong, wise woman and healer, helped those she could in exchange for a ham or a wool coat or the mending of a pot. How much was magic, how much learning, and how much common sense, Hannah Strong never said, but most people left satisfied.

"I have settled the herb garden," Grayling said.

"Have you gathered the herbs as I bid you?"

"Yes," Grayling said, lifting up her basket.

"Did you pull out any bindweed or thistle?"

"Of course."

"By the roots? Nasty things, if you don't."

"Indeed."

"Come in, then, and stir the marsh-mallow root bubbling in the kettle, and don't be letting it burn while you laze. Young George Potter suffers from a clenching of the bowels and needs a tonic."

Grayling nodded and entered the cottage.

"Thomas Middleton will be coming anon with his son Gabe, who suffers from boils. While I lance and clean them, you will watch over Thomas's youngest, for his mother lies abed with melancholy."

"Aye, I will." Grayling clumped her way to the kettle hanging over the fire. "If you say I will, I will," she muttered. "You know I will. *Of course* I will. I always do." When Thomas and his boys arrived, Grayling, as she was accustomed, slipped into the corner, and the little boy dozed on her lap.

Grayling mostly avoided those who came for her mother's remedies, charms, and tonics. Greeting folks meant speaking up, and Grayling thought her mother spoke enough for both of them. And the girl learned many things by listening when visitors forgot she was there.

Margery Atwood wanted a love charm to woo the miller's son away from Cecily Waterstone. Ralph Farquhar had a rash shaped like a turnip on his bum. Randall Pike's pig found its way into Wellington Baker's yard and cooking pot, so Randall Pike perched on Wellington's doorstep and wouldn't move until he was paid for the pig. Randall's wife brought him bread and beer each day at noon, and he voided his bladder in a door-side gooseberry patch.

William Miller had a vision of soldiers marching on the road north of town, and Hannah Strong believed it likely a true sighting, portending conflict, for the land was in turmoil. "Warlords are forming their own armies," she said with a frown. "The powerful want more power, the wealthy want more wealth, and heaven help those who get in their way."

"Aye," said Thomas Middleton. "Them what has, gets, and the rest of us make do with turnips."

"Leastwise," said Hannah Strong with a quick slice at a boil on Gabe's shoulder, "you have turnips, and a home and bed, so you have no need to go to edge dwelling."

"Aye," repeated Thomas Middleton. "I seen them, bullies living rough and menacing them passing by. I say tae you, summat wicked be in the kingdom."

Grayling's skin prickled with unease. There were some things she would rather not have heard.

Next morning, mist again sheltered the valley. Grayling sat cross-legged on the edge of the pond, humming as she scoured the kettle. She thought about dinner. They still had parsnips and carrots in the ground, and perhaps there were enough apples left for an apple tart. With cream, if only they had cream. She licked her lips.

"Grayling, come. Attend me now!" Her mother's voice. The calling mingled with the croaking of frogs in the pond and the *ting-tang* of dewdrops, and it sounded to Grayling like a sort of music.

"Grayling, come at once, or I shall turn you into a toad!" her mother shouted again, much louder. *Belike she would if she could,* Grayling thought. *By borage and bryony, I can do but one thing at a time. Why can she not do whatever it is herself and leave me be?* Hidden as she was in the mist in the herb garden, Grayling could think such things, even though she could not imagine saying them.

She clambered to her feet, left the kettle to soak in the pond, and filled a basket with the remaining watercress and mint that grew at the water's edge. Finally, swinging her basket at her side, she turned for the cottage and her mother.

The mist was clearing elsewhere, but the cottage was still obscured. Grayling drew closer. Everything was the same, yet somehow different. There was the steeply roofed cottage of wattle and yellow-tinted daub. Brass bells still hung from the eaves, and a swag of hazel rods and garlic yet festooned the little window. Smoke poured from the smoke hole in the roof and . . . that was it. Not mist but smoke shrouded the cottage! Too much smoke! Suddenly the roof thatch exploded into flames.

What had happened? Where was Hannah Strong? "Mother!" Grayling screamed. The flames chewed at the little house, but she darted forward. The terrible roaring of the fire hurt her ears, and the heat forced her back. "Madam, my mother!" she screamed again. "Where be you? Answer me!"

"Cease your clamoring, Grayling," Hannah Strong said. "I be right here." The voice was low and hoarse, belike from the shouting and the smoke, but her mother's voice nonetheless. Grayling turned. Her mother stood at the edge of the clearing.

Grayling stumbled over and grabbed her hand. "What has happened? Come, run, before the fire finds the trees and we are lost!" She tugged at her mother's hand. The woman swayed like a sapling in a strong wind but neither followed Grayling nor toppled over. She stood straight and strong and still.

Still? Grayling's mother was never still. She was all color, bustle, and fuss, wrapped in crimsons and blues and the gold of the mustard paste served with sausages at the Unicorn's Horn. There came a quivering in Grayling's chest as if a flock of the grayling butterflies for which she was named were imprisoned there, and her face grew cold with fear.

"Why do you stand here, Hannah Strong?" she asked, her voice atremble. "Why do you not move? Come away with me, do!"

"Witless child, open your eyes and look," her mother said, pulling her hand away and gesturing toward her feet. They were rooted into the earth. What had been toes were now spreading roots, and what had been soft skin was as rough and brown as a tree trunk.

"Oh, monstrous!" Grayling said in a rough whisper. She dropped to the ground and clawed at the bark on her mother's feet. "Who did this? And why?"

Hannah Strong put her hand on Grayling's shoulder. "Enough, enough. 'Twill do no good." She shook her head, and dark hair fell across her face. "I know not the who or the why. Destruction came as smoke and shadow, fired the house, and left me as you see me."

"What are we to do?" Grayling cried over the pounding of her heart.

Her mother shook her head again.

Grayling stood and wiped her hands on her skirt. She could not move for terror and barely breathed as she watched the progress of the flames. Her mother did not know. Her mother — wise woman, hedge witch, purveyor of potions to heal and to cheer; who had charms and spells and power; who was the wisest and surest and strongest person Grayling could imagine — did not know. Grayling felt a clenching in her belly and in her heart, and her hands shook.

No sound reached her ears but for the roaring of the fire — no twittering of birds, no chatter of squirrels or hooting of owls, no singing of the frogs by the pond. The flames finally took the cottage and the apple tree beside but went no farther.

After a time, what remained had cooled enough for Grayling to draw closer. The roof was gone, she saw, and the walls, though standing in some places, were burned through in others. She took a hawthorn stick to protect against evil and poked in the char and the ashes.

Her mother's clay jars, pots, and crocks of salves and potions were buried in ash. Some were broken, their contents spilled. Others were whole, dingy with soot, and still warm to the touch. Cooking pots were blackened, candlesticks melted into pools of tin. The two chairs by the hearth were gone, as were the beams heavy with drying herbs and the spinning wheel in the corner.

"Fetch my grimoire from beneath the hearthstone," Hannah Strong called. "Bring it to me. There may be answers within."

Yes! The grimoire! Likely the book of chants and spells and rituals, passed from mother to daughter to daughter to daughter over generations — nay, over centuries — would reveal some way to undo the magic rooting her mother in the ground. Grayling could only hope it would. She had never seen inside the book. Her mother guarded it carefully.

Grayling picked her way through the debris to the fireplace. With some effort, she lifted the stone, then dropped it down again. There was no grimoire there, just a dank and dirty hole.

"Your *pharmika* is in shambles, lady," Grayling said when she had stumbled back to her mother, "and the grimoire is gone."

"Toads, rats, and dragons," Grayling's mother muttered. "Belike that is what it came for, the demon or force or whatever it was."

Grayling gestured to the ruins of their home. "Why would someone who could do *this* need your book of spells?"

"I do not know, but we must discover the *how* and the *how not* afore I leaf out to my fingertips. Since I am at the moment confined to this place, you must go. Find the others, if it is not too late. Tell them what has happened here, seek their counsel, discover some way to release me. And find my grimoire."

Grayling's heart thumped. "I cannot. You know the world out there be strange and dangerous, and I have no magic and very little courage." She pulled at her mother's sleeve. "Bethink you on it. There must be something you can do. Folk who come to you for remedies and spells always leave contented."

The wise woman frowned at her daughter. "I can do nothing, go nowhere, rooted to the ground as I am. You will have my philters and potions, my charms and my songs, the wisdom of the others, and your own wits."

Grayling shook her head *no* and *no* again. "Your philters and potions are burned and scrambled, the charms and songs are yours and not mine, I do not know of any *others*, and my wits? You have often called them weak and fragile things."

"Although it appears your tongue works exceedingly well. Now hush and let us tackle the impediments one by one." Grayling's mother sighed. "How I wish I could sit down. My knees pain me with the standing." Her eyes filled with dark sadness, and Grayling's heart grew sore with sorrow and fear. "Bring me the witch hazel and comfrey ointment."

Grayling gestured toward the ruins of the cottage. "Everything is tumbled and broken, spilled and charred and ruined. I don't know what is what or for which."

"Go and fetch what jars survive. We can know the contents by their smell."

Grayling went back into the remains of the cottage. With her hazel stick, she poked through the debris again and lifted the pots that were most whole. She wrapped them in her skirt, carried them back to her mother, and laid them at the woman's feet . . . roots . . . feet. One by one, the girl lifted the vessels and took a deep sniff of the contents. Some burned her nose, some comforted it, some made her belly turn over in distress, but they all smelled alike to Grayling—"Like smoke and loss," she told her mother.

The comfrey ointment could not be found, but Hannah Strong could identify the rest. "The one with a faint scent of roses and lovage is the binding potion to compel faithfulness," she said, and, "*Achoo!* That is sneezewort to repel insects." She named them all. Grayling ripped pieces from her shift, covered each pot with a scrap, and tied it on with twine. Then, at her mother's instruction, she marked its name with a piece of charred wood, for Hannah Strong thought a wise woman's daughter should know the way of words. The pots went into Grayling's basket: potions and salves and oils for protection, for sleeping and healing, for binding, shape shifting, and truth telling.

"With these you will not be defenseless. Now go," her mother said. "You needn't fight any demons or dragons. Just find the others, if others there still be."

"Who or what are these *others?*"

Hannah Strong waved a hand about. "Hedge witches, hags, charmers and spellbinders, conjurers, wizards, and soothsayers. You do not think I am the only cunning woman in the world? We be solitary folk, but they will come when you call."

Grayling backed away, shaking her head. "Such a task calls for a brave and skillful person, someone bold, with cunning and magic. Call on one like that."

"Daughter, you say enough *no* for a town full of faint hearts," said Hannah Strong. She would have stamped her foot in irritation if foot she'd had. "Would I had a spell to compel you, but I must rely on your care for me." Hannah leaned over and rubbed her right knee. She was bark to her shins.

Grayling felt the rush of a familiar combination of overwhelming love for her mother, annoyance at her demands, and fear of her temper, her power, her determination. She paused to think. Belike she could find one of these *others*, one with magic and skill, who might know what to do and do it, and she could come home. It might be that simple.

"How would I find these others?"

"Go to the market square of a town, as many towns as there be, and sing."

"Sing? Sing what?"

"There is a gathering song I will teach you. Sing

this, and the others, if others there still be, will find you." Hannah Strong, her knees brown and rough as bark, sang.

By wax and wick,
By seed and root,
Through storms of trouble,
We gather.

Strange matters appear:
Thunder and fog,
Dark and midnight hags,
Toads, beetles, bats
Surround us.

From town and country, hill and valley,
From mountain's snowy crest,
From cellar, attic, church, and alley,
I call to you. I call to you.

Afore danger find us, shackles bind us,
And dreams go up in smoke.
Come to me, come to me,
All wise and cunning folk.

Come—
By wax and wick,

By seed and root,
Through storms of trouble,
We gather,
We gather.

Grayling brightened. "Have you now called them with the song? Will they come here and tell us what to do to free you?"

Hannah Strong shook her head. "It will be many miles and many singings before they will hear and respond. But they will, if any there be — there is power in the song. Now *you* sing."

All unwilling, Grayling sang, stumbling over the unfamiliar words, again and again until she knew the song. Then her mother taught her a song to sing to the grimoire and how to listen for the grimoire singing back, provided that no water stood between them.

There were three kinds of songs, Grayling knew — a song with words and music, a song with melody and no words, and a song with no words and no melody that was instead a thrumming in the head and a throbbing in the heart. This last was what her mother taught her now, and Grayling heard it not with her ears but with her mind and her spirit. And she repeated it the same way.

"But do not sing to the grimoire until you find the others," Hannah Strong said. "You will need their assistance and support."

The sun was setting behind the trees, shafts of golden light piercing through the greenery, before the teaching was finished. Grayling took the basket of herbs, bottles, and pots and added the hawthorn stick against evil, a wool winter cap with earflaps, and half a loaf of bread toasted but not consumed by the fire. She slipped a piece of angelica root into her pocket for protection. Her mother, not one for hugging, patted her on her back.

"Mayhap," Grayling said in a small, thin voice, "I should wait until morning and start fresh on the road."

Hannah Strong said, in a voice as soft but strong as silk thread, "You are the wise woman's daughter. 'Tis up to you to set this right. Go."

Grayling pulled her cloak tight about her. She left her mother there in the valley and ventured forth on her own, reluctant and frightened, up the rise.

I I

hen twilight turned to dark and clouds scudded across the moon, Grayling fell asleep in the hollow of an old oak, cushioned by fallen leaves and moss. The songs of sparrows and thrushes and soft-voiced doves woke her shortly after dawn, and she shivered, both from the early morning chill and from the memory of what had happened. The smell of the fire was yet in her nose and her hair and her clothes, the terrible image of her mother rooted to the ground in her mind and her heart. How was she to go on? She didn't even know where she was.

Grayling sat up, rubbed dewdrops from her face with the hem of her skirt, and looked about for something familiar. She knew every inch of the valley, every path that twisted and turned through the forest, every tree, every clearing, every stream. But here, up the rise? Here she knew nothing.

She had sometimes been to a town but never by herself. She had merely followed her mother as she shopped, visited, and tended. Which was the road to the nearest town? Grayling wondered. What would she find there? And how did her mother fare? Mayhap she should go back and see . . .

A scritching in the grass startled her, but it was only a mouse, sitting near her basket, cleaning its paws with a tiny pink tongue. Her basket! Grayling let forth a squeal and held her hand over her heart. The basket had been overturned, and the pots were cracked and broken. And empty. The pots were empty. Her only defense against the evil that came as smoke and shadow was gone.

"Who has done this?" Grayling cried, her heart pounding as she looked wildly about her. She saw no one. "You, mouseling, are the only witness," she told it. "How I wish you could talk and tell me how this happened."

The mouse ceased its preening and twitched its bounteous whiskers. "This mouse must declare, girl with gray eyes . . ." It hiccoughed. "This mouse must declare, it spilled the jars and ate what they contained."

Grayling squealed again. "You are talking? Or do I still sleep? I must still sleep and dream."

"This mouse is most astonished, mistress, but it is talking indeed. It was an ordinary mouse one moment, and you wished it could talk, and now it can."

Grayling understood. "The wishing potion!" she said. "You ate the wishing potion!"

"'Tis likely. This mouse ate a great many things." The mouse burped a tiny burp and looked up at Grayling. "Ah, Gray Eyes, be kind. This mouse is yours and pledges to stay by you and serve you always."

"And the binding potion also!"

The mouse clambered onto her lap. "Tell this mouse what you would have it do for you."

Grayling stood. The mouse tumbled to the ground, where it shook and shivered and became a frog. "*And* the shape-shifting tonic! You foolish creature, you have left me defenseless."

The mouse appeared again for a moment and then the frog was back. "Shape shifting? This mouse finds it strange and a little frightening but quite stirring," it said. "Mistress Gray Eyes, this mouse loves you and will never leave you." And the frog became a goat with two horns and a beard that waggled as he chewed.

Grayling's head swam in anger and confusion. Even so, she could not help but find it funny. A shape-shifting mouse. Whoever could have imagined such a thing? "You silly thief! The jar held enough shape-shifting potion for a giant of a man, and 'twas eaten by one small, ridiculous mouse. Or goat. Or whatever you be. Likely you can expect much adventure to come."

She plopped herself back down on the ground, her legs curled beneath her. A girl and a shape-shifting mouse against the fury that could fire a cottage and curse Hannah Strong? Grayling was certain her efforts would come to nothing, but she could not go back to watch her mother become a tree. The other wise folk—the hedge witches and charmers and cunning women—certes they would know what to do. If she could find them.

Towns, Hannah Strong had said. Many towns. "Know you the way to a town?" Grayling asked the goat.

The goat shook its shaggy head. "This mouse may look like a goat, but within, it is still a mouse," the goat said in a voice still distinctly mouselike. "This mouse knows only what mice know: eat, sleep, mate, and run away."

It was up to her. "Well, then, I say we go this way," she said, pointing. "This path leads down, which is easier than going up. My legs still pain me after yesterday's climb." Grayling ate her bread, then considered her basket. But for her winter cap, it now held only wilting herbs and a few empty and broken pots and jars. Should she trouble herself to carry it with her? It spoke to her of home, so she grasped it tightly and got to her feet.

She looked one last time down the hill to her valley. There was mist on the treetops, but still she could see their herb garden and, through the trees, a peek at the ruins of their cottage. She blinked to banish her tears, squared her shoulders, and turned away.

The girl with the basket and the goat took the path down. Sunshine caressed the soft hills, their green now marked with autumn's browns and golds. It would be a good day, Grayling thought, for weaving straw into hats or finding honeycombs or watching her mother brew a rose-petal tonic to calm the belly. It was not at all a good day for being brave, going into a town and singing, and battling powerful, mysterious beings.

The path was dusty and deserted, and her footsteps padded on the soft earth. The goat, snacking on thistles and thorns, followed.

As the day wore on, the sun grew warm, and Grayling, grown drowsy, tripped over a tree root and stubbed her toe. *I knew 'twas an unsound, unwise, daft, and doltish decision sending me,* she thought. *I cannot even walk to town without bumbling.* But what if her mother knew that Grayling had some hidden power, unknown to Grayling herself, and that was why Hannah Strong had sent her? What if she could shake her hair, and flowers would appear in her path, or wave her hand, and sausages be brought her, or snap her fingers, and her mother be released? Would that not be splendid? She shook her hair like a pennant, waved her hand, and snapped her fingers, but nothing happened, and Grayling walked on, limping a bit and grumbling.

Around a corner they happened upon a party of children, young enough to be cocky and hotheaded and old enough to make trouble. Grayling froze, and she held tightly to the angelica root in her pocket.

"Hie, girl. Give us your coins!" a boy shouted. He

grabbed one arm just as another boy grabbed the other, and they pushed and pulled her back and forth between them. She tripped and stumbled and fell to the ground, and the boys danced around her.

The biggest boy seized her basket. "Have you coins in there? Or food? Give it here." He pulled her wool cap onto his head with a grin and searched the basket for something valuable. Finding only herbs and broken pots, he cursed and swung the basket away.

"Look, a goat!" a girl shouted as that animal, still munching, drew near. "Supper! Hist, Barnaby! Make the stew pot ready!" She grabbed the goat by the neck. Irritated by her roughness, the creature changed into a cat, spitting and scratching, before becoming a goat once again.

There was a sudden silence before the biggest boy whispered, "How did you that?"

Grayling shook her head. "'Twas not me," she said. "'Tis just that the mouse ate a potion . . ." The boys were not listening. They pulled Grayling to her feet and closed in on her and the goat.

"Barnaby! Caratacus! Philby!" the biggest boy called. "Magician! We have caught us a magician!"

"And a goat," the girl added.

A big man with a big grin and very big hands emerged from a grove of trees. "Well done, striplings," he said in a thick and throaty voice. "It shall be goat for dinner. And a magician, you say? This silvery sprite of a girl? If 'tis true, we shall make good use of her." He grabbed the goat by a horn and Grayling by an arm and, though they wriggled and wraxled, pulled them into the woods.

A number of folk were camped in the shadows, and Grayling shivered to see them. Their weasel-brown tunics and cropped hair marked them as the edge dwellers Thomas Middleton had spoken of—vagabonds and petty thieves who loitered at the outskirts of towns and like gnats bedeviled travelers to and from. She held tighter to her angelica root and wished fervently that she had a hare's foot or anything else with stronger magic.

The big man shoved Grayling and the goat toward a frazzle-haired woman sitting before a tattered tent of felted wool. "Tie them up hereabout," he said.

She grinned a toothless grin and pulled a knife from her belt. "Goat stew! I can make it at once. Fetch a pot and three onions!"

The boy in Grayling's cap spoke up. "We did see it

change into a cat for a moment and back again to goat. Do you think it safe to eat, or be it devil ridden?"

The big man shrugged. "Kimper will know," he said. "We will wait and ask Kimper when he returns." And that was that. Grayling and the goat were tied to a tree and left while the edge dwellers sat and shared bread and beer.

Who might this Kimper be? Were he as big and rough as the others, Grayling's quest was over already. She pulled at her ropes but to no avail.

The goat nudged Grayling's arm. "Does this mouse get nothing to eat?" he asked. "I am hungry as a . . . a . . . a goat."

"You ate your way here," she said, "while my belly aches with emptiness." *In truth, it is more likely fear and vexation. Captured and imprisoned on my first day!* Tears began to carve a path through the dust on her face.

The edge folk ate and drank their fill and then, shouting and laughing, in such a mood as in other folk might call for songs and dancing, they retired to a clearing for wrestling, stabbing with sharp sticks, and caving in skulls with cudgels.

Again Grayling struggled against the ropes that

bound her to the tree. "See what you have done with your shape shifting, you stupid creature," she muttered to the goat. "Would that I had never seen you, that the potions you ate had sickened you, that you would go away and trouble me no more."

"Alas, Gray Eyes, this mouse is bound to you."

"Then I fear more trouble is to come." And there was silence.

The shadows grew longer and the day dimmed as Grayling fell into an uneasy sleep, dreaming of goats changing into trees and Hannah Strong becoming a mouse and Grayling herself, helpless and screaming in a stew pot. She was awakened by the squeaking and rustling of some small creature. "Mouseling, is that you or a real mouse?" she whispered as she wiggled and stretched her aching limbs.

"This mouse *be* a real mouse." Grayling felt a gnawing at the bonds on her ankles. "The shape shifting took it again, and the rope that held a goat proved too loose for a mouse. Now this mouse is free, and you will be too."

"Do hurry, mousie," Grayling whispered, "afore they come back. They would have eaten the goat, and I believe they would consider eating me also." She wiggled, hoping to break through the nibbled ropes. "Why could you not change into a knife or a hand ax?"

The mouse continued chewing, and Grayling continued wiggling. The edge dwellers were still in the clearing, punching and pummeling each other, when, over the ruckus, she heard someone say, "Kimper comes soon. He will be pleased to see what we have caught for supper."

Kimper? Now! She had to get free now! Grayling gave a final, frantic pull, and the rope snapped where the mouse had chewed. She struggled to her feet, which were stiff and somewhat numbed from being bound. Gathering up her skirt, she fled into the growing darkness, with the mouse scampering after her.

The rising moon, as full as a flower, played hide-and-seek with Grayling as it darted behind the clouds and out again. Crashing into trunks and ducking under branches, she made her way through the trees to the road, where the mouse, breathing heavily, caught up with her. "This mouse will come with you, Gray Eyes," it said between pants. "This mouse might yet be of more service to you."

"Doubtful," she whispered, "but still . . ." She searched the road for her discarded basket. "Here 'tis." She dropped the mouse into the basket and ran as fast as her shaking legs would let her. *They will not catch me and make a mouse-and-Grayling stew,* she vowed. *They will not!*

When the edge-dwellers' camp was far behind them, Grayling found a spot off the road for a rest. The mouse climbed out of the basket, bits of watercress stuck to its chin. "I see you have had your supper," Grayling said. "I would scold you for eating while I ran, but you did save us back there, mousie, so I will not." She stopped and thought a minute. "I cannot always call you *mousie,* for you are at times a goat and even a frog, and I know not what is yet to come. Because you rescued me through your shape shifting, I shall call you . . ." She closed her eyes in thought. "Pook. I shall call you Pook."

The mouse cleaned the remaining bits of herbs from its whiskers. "Pook? Was he too a mouse?"

"Nay. Pookas are fairies, stubborn and annoying but most able shape shifters."

Pook sighed. "How this mouse loves to hear you speak, Gray Eyes."

Grayling snorted. How many folks could say they were admired by a mouse?

Darkness fell. It frightened Grayling a bit but also made her feel safer, hidden from anyone following. "I want to go home," she whispered, but truly she now had no home. The cottage was gone, and her mother was becoming a tree. She snuggled into the roots of an ancient oak as if they were a mother's arms, and at last she slept. And the mouse watched over her.

I I I

orning found Grayling, with a mouse asleep in her basket, on the out-skirts of a town. Early as it was, folks had gathered to buy and sell, haggle and quarrel, barter and bargain and steal. There were masters looking for servants and ser-vants for masters, young women in search of husbands and young men with anything but marriage on their minds, fortunetellers and fortune seekers, horses and horsemen, shepherds and sheep. Stalls brimmed with apples and parsnips and fresh brown bread, silken laces

and amber bracelets, woolen hats and wooden spoons. Never had Grayling been alone among so many things and so many people, so many colors and sounds and scents.

An old woman in russet with a basket of onions strapped to her back pulled on Grayling's skirt. "Ain't you the wise woman's daughter?" the old woman asked. "I seen you with her once. She did help my granny with a cramping in the bowel. Where be she?"

"Not here," said Grayling.

"Likely to be?"

Grayling remembered the rough, brown bark of her mother's legs and shook her head. "Nay, not likely. Not likely at all." She turned to leave, but the woman tightened her hold.

"Be you wise, then? Belike you can help me. I have a wart here on my heel. Hurts summat fierce when I walk."

A young woman standing nearby heard and approached them. "You be a wise woman?" She looked down at the ground as she spoke. "I have me overmuch sorrow. Woe, oh, woe. Can you cheer me?"

"And me," said a gnarled old soldier with watery eyes and a crooked nose who stopped beside them. "I worry, worry, worry. Have you a charm or spell to stop the worries?"

"No, no, and no," said Grayling, backing away. "I have no magic, charms, or spells. I am but the wise woman's daughter."

"What *do* you have?" asked one listener.

"And what *can* you do?" asked another.

Grayling chewed on her lip in thought. She performed easy tasks — she could gather herbs and make a stew when there was meat, light the candles, and strain the beer. But what could she do to *help* folk? "My mother has a healing song —"

"She ain't here, you said," said the woman with the wart.

"Aye. Still, I've heard her sing it many a time. Mayhap I can recall it," Grayling said. She took a deep breath and, shy and uncertain, began to sing, her voice soft and quavering:

> *Earth and Mars,*
> *Moon and stars,*
> *Orbs that fill the sky —*
>
> *Spider webs and*
> *Beetle heads,*
> *Beasts that creep and fly —*

Heavenly orbs go by,
Spirits of creatures come nigh.
Bring healing from woe, from pain, from ills,
Let trouble like wind blow by.

"Is that all? What use is a song?" her listeners called, but one of them said, "Sing it again."

So she did, louder and with fewer quavers.

The old man patted Grayling's shoulder. "Hearing your sweet voice, I forgot my worries for a while."

"And I believe my sadness is less," said the young woman with a very small smile.

The two left. Grayling's heart gave a happy jump. Could it be she had the skill, the power, the magic, to heal with a song?

The woman with the wart unstrapped the basket of onions from her back, sat, and removed her shoe. She rolled down a stocking more dirt than wool and pulled it away from her heel. The wart remained, large and red. She shook her head. "Belike the others were not healed but merely cheered by the singing," she said.

"Belike," said Grayling, and her shoulders slumped. "I have no magic, no healing spells, and no wart charms. I cannot help you."

The woman frowned and raised a grimy fist.

Magic or no magic, Grayling would have to do something to avert evil signs or painful thumps. She reached into her basket, pulled out a broken jar with scraps of ointment that had escaped the mouse, and sniffed it. *Sharp,* she thought, *whatever it is. Strong. Mayhap potent.* "Here, take this," she said to the woman with the wart. "Apply a drop every morning at dawn for seven days, and your wart will disappear." *By which time, I trust I will be far, far away.*

The woman smelled it, and her nose twitched. "What is it?"

"My mother's wart-removing tincture, handed down from granny to granny." *Or mayhap a tonic against coughing or a love potion or spiced plum compote for Sunday supper.* "Take it."

The old woman tossed the jar into her basket. "I have no coins," she said, crossing her arms.

"Then it be a gift."

She, too, left satisfied.

Grayling sang the gathering song in a small voice that grew a bit stronger as she ended:

> *Come —*
> *By wax and wick,*

By seed and root,
Through storms of trouble,
We gather,
We gather.

Curious folk stopped to listen, and one prosperous-looking merchant threw her a copper, but they drifted away when the song was finished, and no one approached to ask what she was about.

When Grayling left that town for another, Pook the mouse was still with her, and on they went. Some towns smelled like warm bread, others like wet dogs and old boots. Some were crowded with farmers and merchants and soldiers, and some were no more than tumbledown inn, dung heap, and swarm of starveling cats.

She was still wary of the unknown world outside her valley, and she missed her mother, but she pressed on day after day. She earned what coins she could for tending a toddler, unloading a wagon, or watching over a stall, so she did not go hungry—or, leastwise, very hungry. She dropped bits of food into her basket or her pocket for Pook, who stayed safely hidden, for towns were too busy and crowded for a shape-shifting mouse. They slept wherever it was softest and driest and safest. In each town, she sang the gathering song, softly and tentatively, but no one was summoned ... until at last, someone was.

I V

here was thunder, and gusts of wind, and rain had begun as a drizzle when Grayling, with Pook huddled in her pocket, reached the market square of yet another town. Her hair dripped, her feet squelched in her soggy shoes, and her cloak was growing sodden. She found a place to stand under a tree near the blacksmith's forge and toasted her back at his fire.

"Be it you who calls me?" asked a voice. Grayling turned. A woman stood there studying her, an old woman with a face as wrinkled as a raisin and grizzled hair poking from beneath a linen veil and wimple.

The drizzling rain became a downpour, and the woman joined Grayling under the shelter of the tree. "Be it you who calls me?" she asked again, shaking the rain from her broom of heather and hazel. "I have followed the singing for some days now."

Could it be? "Are you one of *the others?*" Grayling asked.

"Perchance," said the old woman a mite peevishly.

Grayling searched the wrinkled face for some encouragement behind the peevish but, finding only more peevish, took a deep breath and spoke. "Smoke and shadow fired our cottage, left my mother, Hannah Strong, rooted to the ground, and took her spell book, so she sent me to find others, if others there still be, to break the curse and discover what is afoot, but I am fearful and already was captured, and the goat also, so the mouse—"

"Slow, child, slow. You gibber like a gaggle of grouse, and my ears don't hear as fast as once they did." The old woman dashed raindrops from her face with her sleeve. "Like simmering soup, stories cannot be hurried. Tell me everything that befell you, but tell it slow." So Grayling did, ending her tale with a fluttering sigh.

The woman shook her head, and her chin wobbled above her wimple. "Alas, I have seen it. Hovels and cottages and manors afire, cunning women and mages and hags transformed, spell books taken."

Grayling's skin prickled with unease. So others besides her mother were spellbound. Was it everywhere?

"I agree with Hannah Strong," the old woman continued. "'Tis likely that the malevolent force is after the grimoires. But what it wants with them, I do not know." She shook her head again. "I be Auld Nancy, and it may be you and I are all the cunning folk left. Two of us against smoke and shadow. 'Twill not be a fair fight."

"We are three," came a whisper. "I am here too." From behind a gooseberry hedge, a plump young girl in a russet tunic and striped stockings showed herself. Below her linen cap, her fine yellow hair hung stringy and wet, and a few drops dribbled from her cold-reddened nose.

"Yes, Pansy, you are here too." The old woman rolled her eyes skyward and muttered to Grayling, "Her mother, my niece, is most exasperated with the girl and asked me to look after her for a bit. Blanche is the county's most renowned reader of palms, but she says she can teach the girl nothing, awkward as she is, and foolish, and sullen."

Pansy drew closer. Her face was as white and puffy as risen bread dough, and Grayling thought that if she poked it with her finger, the poke would remain. Pansy wiped her nose on her sleeve and looked down at her feet. *Poor girl*, Grayling thought. *I know what it is like to have a mother who thinks you lacking.*

The old woman coughed softly before raising her voice again. "Now, I need me a mug of honey mead and a sausage bun ere we talk more."

"I see an inn," said Grayling, pointing across the square.

"*Hmmph*," said the old woman. "'Tis likely crowded with folks escaping the rain." To Grayling's amazement, Auld Nancy plucked an ember from the blacksmith's forge with her fingertips. Chanting deep and low, words and sounds Grayling could not identify, the old woman tossed the ember into the air and shook her broom. At once the rain stopped, the clouds moved on, and a sun like summer fired the sky.

Grayling's jaw dropped. Auld Nancy had magic! Were it for good or ill? Grayling peered into the woman's face. She did not look wicked or harmful, just old and sour. Did her magic extend only to banishing rain? Or could she be the one to unroot Hannah Strong and vanquish the evil that came as smoke and shadow?

"I am not that kind of witch," said Auld Nancy, as if she read Grayling's thoughts. "Folks call me weather witch, but I have only homely hedge-witch magic— finding lost dogs and cats, calling forth thunder, ripening fruit, stopping rain, and such." She raised her broom like a battle flag and marched toward the inn, which was rapidly emptying as folks sought the sunshine. "Still, my skills, humble though they be, serve me. We shall have no trouble finding a place to sit now."

They followed her, Pansy tripping over her feet and Grayling trailing after, curious and wary. She had been inside an inn but once, for her mother said, "We may as well spread mustard on our pennies and eat them as give them to an innkeeper."

Behind a tall door bound with hinges of iron, the inn was dim and musty, redolent with the smell of wet wool, old wood, and older dirt. The windows were sooty and begrimed, but lanterns hung from the ceiling and a fire gave off welcome light. The three settled themselves around a table with vacant benches. A small pig was roasting on a spit inside the large hearth. Dripping fat sizzled in the flames, and the aroma drove all worry from Grayling's belly, leaving hunger behind. Auld Nancy produced a handful of copper coins, and sausages, pork ribs, fresh bread, and cool mead were brought to their table.

A gleam of sunshine peeked in as the door opened. The innkeeper scurried over to a tall woman wrapped in shawls and scarves and veils of amethyst and amber and cornflower blue. He bowed and simpered and groveled, and Grayling was lost in wonder. Who was this woman? Someone important, or wealthy, or powerful, belike.

"Enchantress," muttered Auld Nancy, watching. "You cannot trust enchanters. They be cruel and selfish, vessels of trickery, guile, and deceit. Their enchantments do not last, but beware, beware." She took a sip of her mead and then said slowly, "Still, she may know something of the state of the kingdom."

The woman approached their table, her skirts and scarves swirling as she moved, the innkeeper bobbing behind. She pushed aside her veil to speak, and Grayling gasped. Never had she seen someone so lovely, skin as creamy soft and brown as the wings of a new-fledged sparrow, hair a vast dark cloud about her head, eyes as deep with mystery and promise as a summer night sky. Blue designs of moons and stars were inked on her cheeks, and rings of gold twinkled at her ears. Grayling wanted nothing more than to sit near the woman forever. The fire burned brighter, the mead tasted sweeter, the air was fresher, and her companions were more —

"Stop what you are doing at once!" said Auld Nancy, waving her broom at the lovely woman. "Let the girl be." The old woman shook her head. "Enchantress," she muttered. "Can't put it aside for a minute."

The woman pulled her cloak tighter about her and asked Auld Nancy, "Was it you who summoned me? And why?" Her voice was deep and a little rough, like iron cart wheels on a rutted road. Grayling started in surprise; she had expected music.

"'Twas this girl who called." Auld Nancy sat back and waited for Grayling to tell the story, but Grayling yet sat open-mouthed and gawking. Auld Nancy huffed and began. "Something evil, something with stealth and power, has discomfited our fellows, taken their spell books, fired their dwellings. We think it be the spell books the evil force wants. I be Auld Nancy, and I can call sunshine or rain, but I was spared, likely because I have no grimoire." Popping a bit of bread into her mouth, Auld Nancy went on. "Nor do you, I suspect, for you are here."

The woman sat down. "I am called Desdemona Cork, and 'tis true I have no grimoire. Other enchanters have such — books of charms and spells to attract and enchant — but I have no need." She twitched, and the aromas of fresh bread and warm wine, spring breezes and summer flowers, filled Grayling's nose. Her head spun.

Auld Nancy waved the sweet odors away and said, "Then you may be the only one of your kind left unfettered."

"'Tis true? It seems most unlikely. Who are you that I should believe what you say?"

"Misdoubt me, if you will. Go on your way. But consider if I tell the truth, if there is such a force abroad, and it claims the rest of us. Imagine your feet growing into the ground, and bark, thick and rough, moving up from your ankles, over your body, slowly but relentlessly turning you into a tree."

Pansy squealed. With a squirm and a tug, Desdemona Cork pulled her cloak still closer, and said, "Again

I ask, why was I summoned? What do you want with me?"

"We few here," said Auld Nancy, "unskilled and reluctant as we may be, must discover what is afoot, and why, and who is responsible. We will have to work together."

"I do not work together," said Desdemona Cork. "I have never had the need."

Auld Nancy turned red with temper, and Grayling spoke up. "You *must* help. *Everyone* must help. I have seen the horror of my mother, bark to her knees, rooted to the ground, helpless."

"Roots. Bark. Horror. This sounds dangersome," said Desdemona Cork as she helped herself to a pork rib. "I like it not and will have no part of it."

Auld Nancy slammed her hand on the table, and mead sloshed from their cups. "Go, then," she said, "but leave the rib!" And she yanked the meat from Desdemona Cork's hand.

The enchantress stood, then stopped still as the room grew dark and cold. A wind rose outside that rattled the windows and set the inn sign creaking. It whistled down the chimney, shooting flames from the fireplace like an angry dragon in an ancient story. Wisps of smoke writhed and coiled through the room.

Grayling shivered.

Auld Nancy wheezed.

Pansy whimpered.

And Desdemona Cork sat down again. "It seems that something is amiss indeed. What do you propose we do about it?"

"I expect," said Auld Nancy "that the spell or conjuration we need to defeat this evil force can be found in a grimoire." She paused for a sip from her mead cup. "But how to find the grimoires?"

Grayling looked at the others. Auld Nancy shrugged and stared at the table. Desdemona Cork jingled the bracelets on her arm. Pansy took the last sausage, biting it so fiercely that grease shot out like sparks from a bonfire.

Oh, rats and rabbit droppings! It will have to be me. Grayling gritted her teeth. "We can find my mother's grimoire," she said at last. "She has a song she sings, and her grimoire will sing back, if it is not too far away and no water stands between them."

"A discovery song," said Auld Nancy, and she nodded. "Trust Hannah Strong to have such. But she is not here."

Grayling shook her head. "Nay, she cannot leave, rooted as she is, but she taught me the song. 'Tis not an easy song to sing or to hear, but I will try to teach it to you. You can follow it to her grimoire, and I can go home."

She sang, and the grimoire sang back to her. Grayling heard the song, not through her ears but with every part of her. It was in the air—she could hear it without hearing it. She could see it, taste it, feel it. "Do you hear it?"

"Hear what?" the three asked in unison.

Grayling's hopes sagged. She sang again. "Can you sing it?"

They could not. The others could neither sing the song nor hear the grimoire singing back.

Auld Nancy shook her head. "The song and the grimoire belong to you."

"Nay, they are my mother's."

"Can you sing the song?"

Grayling nodded.

"Does the grimoire sing back?"

Grayling nodded again.

"You can sing, and you can hear it singing back. I would say 'tis yours. So, too, the quest is yours. You must lead us to where the grimoires are so we may unravel this mystery and put things right."

Grayling's head ached. She was no leader, neither brave nor eager for adventure. She wanted none of this. She looked around the table at the others. Desdemona Cork was not trustworthy, Pansy knew nothing, and Auld Nancy thought she knew everything but had no answer for this puzzle. What would happen to them if they challenged the evil force?

The wind shrieked and shook the inn, and the door rattled and banged. "This is no natural wind," Auld Nancy said. "I believe strong forces are clashing and fighting for control, and we are caught between."

V

hey slept, four in a bed, in an attic room high under the eaves. Grayling tossed and turned as the wind yowled like a hungry cat trying to get inside.

During the night, with a *grawk* and a *cronk*, Pook the mouse had burst from Grayling's pocket in a flutter of black feathers. After Grayling explained him to her gobsmacked companions, Pook—now Pook the raven—flapped his wings and settled on the window-sill, where he pecked at the glass all night.

Morning was quiet in the inn. The baldheaded

waiter brought bread and honey and peaches from the south, where it was still summer, to their table. Grayling sat with juice running down her chin, waiting for someone to suggest a plan, but no one said a word. Finally she swallowed and asked, "How shall we begin?"

"We?" asked Pansy. "Must I go? They are preparing pigeon pie for supper."

Auld Nancy pinched Pansy's ear. "I am responsible for you, so where I go, you go. We will follow the sound of Grayling's singing grimoire and hope to put an end to this dark witchery."

As Desdemona Cork was too conspicuous, Pansy too afraid, and Grayling reluctant, Auld Nancy went first. She was the surest and the boldest, short of temper but full of vigor. Following Auld Nancy, Grayling thought, would be much like following her mother.

Autumn was upon them. Here and there, leaves struggled to turn color, and the day was cloudy and cool. Grayling sang and cocked her head as she felt the response. "That way," she said, and she pointed to a path up a hill, rutted and muddy and steep.

Off they went into the gray-sky morning, with Pook the raven soaring above them. He gave a shrill cry, dove to the ground, and skidded to a stop, over and over. Pebbles flew before his claws. His shiny beak pecked at sticks, at stones, at worms and beetles, grains of wheat and crusts of bread. Cawing and cronking, he fluttered to Pansy's shoulder and picked at her hair. "Hellborn bird!" she shouted, and off he flew. Silhouetted against the sky, he spread his great wings, twisting and tumbling, drifting then diving then climbing again. If a raven could laugh, Grayling would have sworn he was laughing.

They trudged on. The road wound up and down and around soft hills bedecked with oaks and elms, and Grayling breathed deeply of the crisp air. In the distance, fields lay fallow, awaiting spring planting. *Perhaps*, Grayling thought, *this venture will not be too difficult. My belly is full, there is no rain, Auld Nancy is leading us, and I have naught to do but sing. Perhaps all will be well.*

They walked on, over barren hillsides, through wooded groves, past villages where church bells were tolling. Breezes sang, trees rustled, dogs menaced them, nipping at their heels. Through crossroads and forks, on tracks and trails, paths and byways and lanes, they walked, following Grayling, who followed the grimoire's song.

Pook swooped in to land on Grayling's shoulder. "This Pook must thank you, Gray Eyes," he said, fixing her with his beady black eye, "for your shape-shifting potion has allowed it to see such things as a mouse would never see—haystacks and hillocks, sheep cotes and steeples and streambeds."

"But, Pook," she asked, her forehead furrowed with worry, "what if the potion wears off while you are in the sky? Or you shift suddenly into a squirrel or a cow? Your plummet to earth would be sudden, messy, and likely fatal."

Pook was silent a moment and then shuddered. "Ah, I see." He looked up at the sky and said softly, "This Pook has soared with eagles. No other mouse can say that. It is now content to stay on the ground." He flapped his wings twice and settled down to nap on Grayling's shoulder. She shifted to settle his weight, for a raven was much heavier than a mouse.

Midafternoon they came to a crossroads. To the south the ground rose in green curves up and up. Along the top of the rise marched a line of soldiers. Faint sounds of feet trudging and weapons clanking echoed. Grayling swallowed hard and looked away.

A town could be seen to the north, but the grimoire sang them west. "Makes no matter," said Auld

Nancy, dropping to the ground beneath an ancient elm and mopping her red face with her skirt. "I can go no more, neither to the west nor to the north, not up nor down."

"Auld Nancy," said Grayling with alarm, "are you unwell?" The old woman was so forceful that Grayling believed nothing but grave illness could stop her.

"Nay, I am but spent and weary. I am older than I look." Gray wisps poked out from the woman's wimple, the hairs on her chin trembled, and the skin on the backs of her hands was coarse and freckled. It was difficult to imagine that she could be older than she looked. Grayling's heart thumped once. What would become of them if Auld Nancy could not go on?

With a whoosh and a whoop, Pansy, grown pale and haggard, dropped down beside Auld Nancy. Grayling looked at the heavy clouds above and then at her companions on the ground. Despite the need for hurry, they would go no farther. What should she do? What would Hannah Strong do? Nay, what would she bid Grayling do?

"I will find wood for a fire," Grayling said, "and a bit of a clearing off the road where we can rest."

"And I," said Desdemona Cork, as fresh and lovely as if she had just woken, "am footsore and hungry. I will go now and find me some supper."

Auld Nancy glared at her. "Selfish wench! You would leave the rest of us to eat grass like sheep? Even enchanters, haughty and sly and thoughtless as you are, must have a care for others now and again. 'Tis the rightful thing to do."

Desdemona Cork huffed and blew a strand of dark hair from her face. She stared at Auld Nancy for a moment, blinking her eyes and frowning, and then said, "'Tis not that I do not care about other people, but I find I rarely notice you." She shrugged a lovely shrug.

"Notice us? Notice *me?*" Auld Nancy pointed a gnarled finger at the enchantress. "I am shower breeder, cloud pusher, fog mistress, ruler of the elements, and I can call down rain, constant rain, upon your head now and forevermore! Would you notice me then?"

There was a long pause. Grayling held her breath. Finally Desdemona Cork said, "I agree to provide supper for us all. Will that satisfy?"

Auld Nancy nodded.

"How will you do that?" Grayling asked.

Desdemona Cork twitched her shawls. The air sparkled and smelled of roses. *Of course,* thought Grayling. *Enchantress.*

Traffic was sparse, but now and then horses and carts passed by, and merchants and farmers, peddlers and soldiers and other folk heading from here to there and there to here. A fine gentleman on a gray horse drew near, heading east. Desdemona Cork twitched her shawls, and before Grayling could puzzle out how, the enchantress was seated before the gentleman on the horse, no longer headed east but instead north into town. *Such a useful skill to have, enchanting,* thought Grayling. *If I could enchant someone,* she wondered, *what would I have him do? Bring me cool water? Brush my hair? Roast me a chicken?*

Grayling watched until Desdemona Cork and her admirer disappeared. "Do you think she will come back?" Grayling asked.

"More important, will supper come back?" added Pansy.

So Pansy did have some wits after all. Grayling gave the girl an encouraging smile, but Pansy was once more looking down at her feet, her lips plumped in a pout.

Light rain began. Pook the raven woke, shook drops off his wings, and turned mouse once more. "'Tis quite an experience for this Pook, the shape shifting," he said.

"The tingling and trembling leave it breathless and most exceedingly tired." He climbed into the pocket of Grayling's kirtle and began to snore. She smiled. *I myself have enchanted a mouse, and I find I like the company.*

While Auld Nancy and Pansy rested under the shelter of the tree, Grayling headed into a thick grove to gather fallen wood for a fire. The trees grew close together, and the air was damp and chill. In her valley, the trees reached out to embrace and caress her; here they grabbed at her skirt and pulled her hair. Grayling pushed her way through, picking up small branches and twigs as she went. The air grew darker and colder, and she shivered.

The trees thinned out at last and gave way to a small clearing where a goat feasted upon the remains of a garden. Behind were the tumbled ruins of a hut. A breeze stirred the leaves on the trees with a rustling like the ghostly whispering of dark secrets. Prickles ran down Grayling's back. She peered over her shoulder and around. No one was here. Still she was uneasy, as if she were being watched. She'd been foolish to venture so far from the others.

"You, girl, here, to me!" Grayling jumped. The call

had been more growl than voice. An old woman stood at the edge of the clearing, half hidden in the trees.

"What has happened? Who has done this?" the woman asked. "Was it you, or be you here to release me?" She broke off in a fit of coughing as Grayling went closer.

Before she had taken ten steps, Grayling could see that the woman was not hidden in the trees. She *was* tree, all the way to her chest. Her battered old face reflected both horror and hope, and she waved her arms—not yet branches—in distress.

Grayling's heart stopped and then hammered. Belike the woman was witch or wizard, and the smoke and shadow had come for her grimoire and left her turning tree! Did the evil force loiter still? Grayling could almost feel her own feet hardening and her ankles tingling. She dropped the gathered wood and, trembling and stumbling, crashed her way back through the woods. Behind her she could hear the woman shouting, "Come back, ye hag-born wench! A plague on ye, Mistress Do-nothing! The devil take ye!"

Right she turned, and left, and right again. Where were the others? Where was the road? Which of these trees had been a person, a person like her, like her mother, now a horrid creature of roots and wood and sap? Gasping and heaving, she burst through the forest onto the road where the others awaited.

"An old woman," she said, once she could speak again. "Tree to her chest." It was the stuff of nightmares. Was that how her mother looked now? Or was she tree entirely? Was there any turning back from bark to flesh?

"Aye," said Auld Nancy, "as I told you, I have seen many such. Wise men and cunning women, magicians and wizards, gone to trees. 'Twas a pitiful sight."

Pitiful and ominous and frightful. Grayling dropped down next to Auld Nancy, sitting close enough to feel the comforting warmth of the old woman's body. Seeing the woman becoming tree had made their venture more frightening and more dangerous. Would the smoke and shadow come for them, too, if they meddled? Grayling's toes tingled. What would it feel like, turning into a tree? Would it hurt? Would your feet and your legs know what was happening?

The rain fell harder, and travelers bustled or scampered or huddled within their cloaks. Auld Nancy wobbled to her feet. "Thundering toads!" she shouted to the drenching skies. "I be discomforted enough! Rain, away!" she cried, shaking her broom. And the rain stopped.

Suddenly murmurs swirled in the air like dandelion fluff. *Witch! Weather witch! She who commands the rain!* A young woman with a basket full of kittens quickly backed away, but others pushed forward, eager to secure a favor.

"Our hedge witches and hags are gone," one said, "and we know not where. Will you serve? I wish a warm wind to dry my field."

"Have you other spells?" asked another. "I would curse my brother-in-law."

"The miller!"

"My pig-headed horse!"

Auld Nancy said over and over, "We are not *that* kind of witch," and Grayling pulled her sleeves from grasping hands and shook her head *no no no*. If she had the magic they thought she had, she would see these pestering folks bewitched away, Or turned to stone, or frogs, or geese.

"Make way! Make way!" Blue-coated soldiers in tall buckled boots and iron helmets, with war hammers and sharp swords at their waists, marched toward them, followed by a man mounted on a fine black horse. His sun-darkened face was crisscrossed with angry scars, his mouth was hard and tight, and his nose . . . his nose was silvery, stiff, and shiny. Like metal. Nay, it *was* metal! His nose, lost no doubt in some battle or duel, was now made of metal, fastened to his face with a black leather band. A metal-nosed warlord with a band of bullies. Grayling shuddered and backed away.

He pointed to Auld Nancy, Pansy, and Grayling. "Take these three and chase the rest of the rabble away," he directed his troops in a voice, thought Grayling, that could freeze fingers and toes on a summer day. "I have need of their magic."

"We are not *that* kind of witch," Auld Nancy said again. The soldiers poked at them with their swords and waved branches of holly and bay to protect against evil in case the three women were indeed *that* kind of witch. Grayling could sing to the grimoire, Auld Nancy make weather, and Pansy — well, what could Pansy do? — but they could not overpower a troop of men with horses and weapons. And Desdemona Cork was gone.

A soldier prodded Grayling toward a wheeled cage woven of hazel branches and banded with cold iron, hitched to two tired-looking horses. She kicked at him, but he swung at her with a switch of holly sprigs. The toothed leaves caught her beneath her right eye and left a jagged cut. She yelped as she was shoved into the cage, and her basket was lost behind her.

There came a trembling in her pocket. "Not now, Pook," Grayling whispered. "Anon, but not now." But indeed the mouse leaped from the pocket, shook himself, and became a goat, eyes bulging and beard a-waggle. With a furious bleat, the goat disappeared, and a raven, cronking, soared into the sky.

The soldiers stared at Grayling a moment and then backed away, waving their holly branches fiercely. Auld Nancy snorted. "We are not that kind of witch," she repeated.

Grayling held the hem of her skirt to her bleeding cheek. "Auld Nancy, be there nothing you can do to stop this folly?"

"I can stop and start rain, send clouds scudding away. I have at times even called snow, but how might that be helpful?"

"What if you smote the metal-nosed man with lightning? Were he struck, the rest might run."

"Lightning," said Auld Nancy with a shudder. "I have never been adept with lightning." There was a long pause. Grayling felt a niggle of hope. Finally Auld Nancy said, "I will try, although I fear my skills, while dazzling, are imprecise. I once set fire to a lady's wig, which she cast off, revealing herself bald as an egg."

"Auld Nancy, *please.*"

Auld Nancy began to chant in a rumble so low Grayling had to struggle to catch every word.

> *O spirits of the storm,*
> *Let wind meet clouds*
> *And fire meet earth.*
> *Let a storm spring forth*
> *And shafts of fire come down*
> *To assault our enemy and strike him low.*
> *I call wind and water, earth and fire.*
> *So might it be.*

Dark clouds filled the sky, crashing and slamming into each other, and rain poured down. As Auld Nancy chanted on, jagged streaks of lightning split the sky. Great shafts of blinding light struck a cart full of cabbages, two hay wagons, and a signpost, and set them ablaze with tongues of fire. The soldiers' horses whinnied and scuffled. Thunder crackled, but the rain doused the fires, and the warlord with the metal nose, untouched and unharmed, laughed a laugh that chilled Grayling's heart.

"Take them," he shouted, and the soldiers, hiding behind each other, succeeded in pushing Auld Nancy and Pansy into the cage with Grayling. They closed a wooden door, fastened it with a lock of iron, and turned away.

The company started toward the town, the metal-nosed man on the fine horse in the lead, followed by the horse-drawn wheeled cage carrying Grayling and her companions. After a while they turned off the road onto a broad trail that led up and up and up. The wheels *thump thumped* on the rough and rutted path and clattered over a bridge. Grayling slumped in a corner of the cage as they shook and jounced on the rough road, wondering where they were headed and why.

V I

he company slowed as they passed beneath a towering arch of stone as dark as the start of a nightmare. Night had fallen when they came to a stop. Candles shone from the windows of a great house, but the yard was lit only by the sliver of moon that escaped the clouds.

Grayling stood and pressed her face against the branches that served as the bars of their cage. She could see little in the moonlight, but she could hear the bustle of their arrival. Horses clopped and whinnied and huffed, footsteps rang on stone or squelched in mud, soldiers called back and forth to each other, and no one paid attention to the prisoners.

Thus ends the first day of our trek together, thought Grayling, *captured and caged like dancing bears.* If only Desdemona Cork had not left them! She could have enchanted the soldiers — perhaps even the man with the metal nose, if such could be enchanted. The captives would likely be in a fine house right now, supping on partridge and elderberry wine, instead of in a cage in the cold with their bellies woefully empty.

Then there was silence, until a man's voice said, "You stay here and guard them."

"Why me? Be you afeared of them witches?" another voice asked.

Scuffle, scuffle, Grayling heard, and then there was quiet again except for the snuffling and spitting of the man who had lost the scuffle.

Auld Nancy moved to Grayling's side. "I found a bit of spider web for your cheek," she whispered. She clucked in concern as she gently applied the web to Graylings's cut with her warm hand.

"You," said a voice both cold and stony. "You witches, I have use for your magic."

"We," said Auld Nancy with an impatient sigh, "are not that kind of witch."

The voice came closer, and so did the speaker, the warlord with the nose of metal. He thrust his face against the branches of their cage and shouted, "I need witch magic, and but for you three, I find no witch, no magician, no wizard abroad in the land!"

"Aye, we know," said Auld Nancy. "'Twas an evil force took them, and we think we can set it to rights if you would but free us."

"Free you? Nay! I need gold, and I need more armed men. You will use your spells, your curses, your powers, whatever you possess, to see that I get them." A tiny ray of moonlight shimmered off the tip of his nose, and Grayling shuddered. "I need the Earl of Whetstone's soldiers to turn and run. And the earl himself I wish gone—whether he dies or leaves the kingdom or just, *whoosh,* disappears, it is up to you, but I want him gone." He slowly paced the breadth of the cage and back, his steps echoing through the courtyard like funeral drums. "I want a cloak of invisibility, a binding spell, and an assortment of poisons that act quickly and surely."

Auld Nancy stamped her foot. "You do not listen. We do not have such powers and cannot—"

The man slammed his hand against the branches of their prison. "You will do as I tell you, or you will remain caged like monkeys until the flesh falls off your bones." He stalked off, shouting over his shoulder, "You will have no food nor drink until I get what I want. And if you remain stubborn, I will have you disemboweled, one by one."

There was a short silence, and then, "I'm frightened," Pansy said with a snuffle, "and terribly hungry. What do we now?"

"At the moment, there is nothing *to* do," said Auld Nancy. "We are at that man's mercy, may maggots build nests in his hair!"

Grayling considered their situation. Likely her mother would know what to do or rather what to tell Grayling to do, but her mother was partway to being a tree. Roots and rutabagas! Grayling herself would have to think of something. In frustration she shook the sides of the cage.

"Gray Eyes," said a voice from above. A raven had landed on the roof of the cage. "Gray Eyes," it repeated, "this Pook is with you. Is there aught he can do?" With a cronk and a shaking of his feathers, the raven became a mouse again. He fell through the bars of the cage and landed with a tiny *ooof!* at Auld Nancy's feet.

Auld Nancy studied him. "Can you not change into something useful — a strong knife, mayhap, or a torch?"

"Or a joint of beef?" asked Pansy.

Ignoring them both, Pook asked again, "Gray Eyes, is there aught that this Pook can do for you?"

"Certes," said Grayling, wiping her eyes on her sleeve. "I wish to be gone from here! How will you make that happen?"

After a moment of silence, the mouse said, "There are two things this Pook might do. One, turn himself into a mad bull and tear down this cage. Two, this mouse can remain a mouse and chew through it."

"Oh, Pook, you *can* help me! Which will you do?"

More silence. "This mouse is compelled to tell the truth. He does not in fact know how to change into a mad bull, so he shall immediately commence chewing. A hole large enough for you to climb through should take" — the moon reflected in the mouse's tiny eyes as they shifted this way and that around the cage — "a month or so."

"A month? Oh, mousie, a month? 'Twill not do. We will be long dead ere a month has passed." Grayling slumped against the cage.

"Nay, mistress, do not despond," said the mouse. "Trust this mouse and wait here." And he skittered away. Grayling smiled through her tears. *Wait here? Where else?*

The three sat together on one side of the cage. Grayling huddled against the warmth that was Auld Nancy, comforted by the familiar aroma of sweat and smoke and sausages. The others dozed, but Grayling, plagued with visions of disemboweling, could not rest.

Some time had passed when she heard a sound, the sound of the wind stripping the grain on a wheat field, or a thousand tailors scissoring cloth, or . . . or . . . or an army of mice chewing through hazel branches — *chiff chiff, chiff chiff, chiff chiff!*

She peered through the darkness. Indeed mice beyond counting were at the other side of the cage, tumbling over each other, gnawing and tearing their way through the branches that served as bars. The noise grew louder as their number grew. *Chiff chiff, chiff chiff, chiff chiff.*

Auld Nancy woke and assessed the scene. "'Tis well done, mouse," she said, "but let us make some noise to drown out the chewing lest the guard hear."

Pansy yawned and said, "Can you not call thunder and lightning?"

Auld Nancy shook her head. "Nay, nothing that would bring attention to us or illuminate what is happening. Nay."

"My mother," said Grayling, "has a song with *chiff chiffs* that she sings as she slashes chive blossoms from their stems. We could sing it loudly."

The mice chewed on. *Chiff chiff, chiff chiff, chiff chiff!*

"What be that sound?" called the guard. "What are you doing in there?"

"We," Grayling said, "are but singing a song with much *chiff chiff, chiff chiff, chiff chiff*ing."

"*Chiff chiff, chiff chiff,*" sang Auld Nancy. She knocked Pansy with her elbow, and the girl shouted, *"Chiff chiff!"*

"I do like a song," said the guard. "Sing so I can hear."

So Grayling sang:

> *Do not go to the field, my girl, today.*
> *'Tis August and the men are cutting hay.*
> *Chiff chiff, chiff chiff*
> *Go silvery scythes.*
> *Harvest is underway*
> *And I wish you would*

Not go to the field today.
Chiff chiff, chiff chiff.
Chiff chiff, chiff chiff.

The mice went *chiff chiff, chiff chiff,* Auld Nancy and Pansy sang *chiff chiff, chiff chiff,* but Grayling was silent a moment as she remembered Hannah Strong singing while she snipped greens in the garden. The sun had lit streaks of bronze in her hair and roses in her cheeks, and her fingers were swift and supple.

"You witches be fine singers," their guard called out. "I vow I can hear the sound of the scythes cutting the hay."

Grayling sang louder as she continued her song and the mice continued their *chiff chiff*s.

Her own true love was in the field that day —
His hair was gold and eyes were moonlight gray.
Chiff chiff, chiff chiff
With silvery scythe
He swung but swung astray.
He cleaved her head
And laid it in the field of hay.
Chiff chiff, chiff chiff.
Chiff chiff, chiff chiff.

"*Chiff chiff, chiff chiff,*" shouted Auld Nancy.

"And *swish. Swish swish,*" cried Pansy, her face red with excitement, "and *slash slash!*"

The listening soldier was so stirred that he had begun to *chiff chiff* along. "Finish the song," he called. "What follows? How fares the girl?"

"Poorly," said Grayling, "for she be headless and dead."

"Dead? Nay! That be a poor story and not worth the listening," the guard said, "with a most unacceptable ending." He crossed his arms and, with a huff and a *bah,* walked away.

"Not all endings are happy," said Grayling. And she sang on.

There were other sounds in the darkness: shouts and cries, the calls of soldiers striding through the yard, the grim and doomful echo of their boots. Ere long, the night grew quiet but for the *chiff chiff* of the mice. More songs were needed, but Auld Nancy and Pansy slumbered in a corner.

"Can you not hurry?" Grayling whispered, but to whom? The cold of midnight settled upon her, and she pulled her cloak tighter. She sang her mother's healing song and a love chant and a song to cheer, although it did not cheer her.

She even sang to the grimoire, but there was no answering song. Face spots and flea bites! Had the song lost its magic? Grayling caught her breath but then remembered — a bridge. They had crossed a bridge. Water stood between her and the grimoire. She hoped it was no more than that.

After a time, the mouse hole had grown large enough for a person to pass through. "'Tis done," Grayling whispered as she woke Pansy and Auld Nancy. And Pook? Where was Pook? She could not leave without him, but the mice were so many, crawling and climbing over each other. Gray mice, brown mice, fat mice, and thin — how would she ever find one special mouse? "Pook," she whispered. "Pook, come hither to me," but there was no response, no Pook with his pink nose and pink ears and more whiskers than any mouse truly needed.

"We must go," said Auld Nancy.

"Not without Pook."

"Who?"

"Pook. The mouse. The raven. The goat."

Auld Nancy shook her head. Grayling could not see

it in the dark, but she knew from the *tsk* sound Auld
Nancy made. "He is a resourceful bird . . . mouse . . .
whatever he is, and likely he will find you."

They had to leave. Pook was resourceful indeed.
Grayling took some comfort in that fact, but still her
heart felt empty and sore.

She climbed out of the cage behind Pansy and Auld
Nancy. Making what haste they could, they fought their
way through a hedgerow thick with thorns and thistles
that scratched their faces and snagged their hair. "Thistles and thorns! Begone! Begone!" Grayling shouted, as
she yanked the skirt of her kirtle from the thorns' grip,
leaving a long gash in the skirt.

They crashed through bushes and brush to a path
heading steeply down. With a sharp cry, Pansy fell, twisting her ankle beneath her. She pulled on Auld Nancy's
skirts and almost toppled her, too. "Clumsy girl!" Auld
Nancy hissed. "Can you do nothing right?"

Pansy felt the sting of Auld Nancy's bad temper more
often than the rest of them, Grayling thought, but then
she earned it more often. "Come," said Grayling to the
girl, "lean on me. I am strong enough for the both of us."
Pansy did, and like a two-headed beast, they scuttled away.

VII

A heavy mist obscured the rising sun and darkened the path. Auld Nancy lifted her broom. "I shall banish the mist and let in the morning light."

"Would that not make it easier for us to be followed when our escape is discovered?" asked Grayling. She sighed a sigh that ruffled the hair on Pansy's head and, all unwilling, offered a solution. "I am accustomed to finding my way in the mist in my valley. I could, I expect, lead, and you follow." Grumbling, she took

Pansy's arm and Auld Nancy's hand, and they crept carefully through the mist down the steep and slippery path.

Grayling knew three kinds of mist—gentle mist that wrapped around her like a fine lady's veil, mist thick with drops of moisture like peas in a soup, and a dense mist full of secrets and dangers and foreboding. This mist was neither gentle nor soupy, but menacing and somehow sinister.

After a time she heard the muffled sounds of horses close behind them and then the marching feet of soldiers. She pulled Auld Nancy and Pansy off the path just as a voice she recognized as the metal-nosed warlord's shouted, "Find them! Do not come back without them lest the disemboweling be yours!"

Grayling broke off a stout elder branch and gave it to Pansy for a walking stick. Off the path it would be harder to walk and slower going, but safer. The three crouched low and crept away.

They skittered and stumbled as the terrain descended more sharply. Grayling suddenly lurched sideways and fell to her knees. Or rather one knee, for her other leg was hanging over the edge of a steep drop into the unknown. Her heart was pounding like a rabbit's.

The world was full of dangers, and she was leading others through it. She was watching over them, but who was watching over her? What if she made a mistake? Finally she rose to her feet and, with a brisk shake of her head, continued on down. And the others followed.

As they circled past the outskirts of a town, there came the noise of conflict. Metal sounded on metal, on earth, on wood. "I expect," said Grayling, "that the soldiers have encountered edge dwellers." She, Auld Nancy, and Pansy moved farther off the road.

The ground turned boggy, and Grayling's shoes squelched a soggy sort of tune: *squish squelch, squish squelch.* Ahead was a small grove of trees, saplings, not much taller than she. Their trunks were slender and green, supple and strong, but . . . Grayling gulped. Trees, but yet men! Trees to just below their eyes, and men above. Their arms, lifted as if in supplication, were newly leafed out although it was autumn, and their fingertips waved in distress. With soft moans and sighs, the rustling leaves murmured as if calling for help.

Fear suffused the air like a bad smell. Grayling felt her head spin with panic and revulsion. She turned away and hurried off, whispering, "Sorry, sorry, sorry," for she was useless and as helpless as they were. Auld Nancy and Pansy, picking their way over the marshy ground, noticed nothing.

A slippery bank led down to a rocky, fast-flowing stream. Here was the water that stood between Grayling and the grimoire. They would have to cross it.

Pansy, limping and stumbling in the rear, sneezed a great, noisy sneeze.

"Husht!" said Grayling over her shoulder.

Pansy wheezed.

"Husht!" said Auld Nancy over *her* shoulder.

Pansy gurgled.

Grayling and Auld Nancy turned to look at her. Fie! Someone was there, someone taller than Pansy and bulkier, someone in an iron helmet, someone with his arm tight across Pansy's throat and a sword in his hand.

"You will do as I say, or this wench will find her head separated from her body," the soldier said. "'Tis an oddsome thing. They all be looking for you, and I, who wanted only to run off, stumble across you. Good fortune for me, as Lord Mandrake has promised a reward." He pushed Pansy to the ground. She whimpered as she fell on her injured leg, and her eyes and her nose ran. "Sit and be still," he said to all of them. "We will wait here until those edge-dwelling brutes are routed or destroyed."

They sat, Pansy at his side and his sword at the ready. The mist was heavier here near the water, the air dank and rank with the smell of rotting vegetation, and the ground mucky and cold. Grayling wriggled until she was as comfortable as she was likely to get.

The soldier stretched out his legs. "Make a fire," he commanded. "This blasted damp creeps into my very bones." He removed his helmet and scratched his head.

Auld Nancy pulled a tinderbox from her pocket and removed the flint and the steel striker. She rose and gathered together small twigs and dried leaves, struck the striker against the flint again and again, and blew on the sparks. Soon there was a tiny fire, which Grayling fed with fallen branches, and the two sat again.

Grayling watched the fire flicker. What could be done to free Pansy? Free all of them? "I have been pondering what to do about this lout," she muttered softly to Auld Nancy. "Might you call lightning down upon him and toast him to a cinder?"

"Aye, I might," Auld Nancy said. "But I might miss and toast you or Pansy, fire a tree or nothing at all. You have seen how imperfect are my skills with lightning. He would be alerted and likely angry."

Grayling wiggled her feet as she thought. Could *she* do something? She knew about straining beer and spinning wool, finding firewood and gathering herbs. Herbs. Certain herbs were known to cause deep sleep. Was there sleepy nightshade or valerian nearby? She looked about her by the light of the fire but saw none. There were mint, watercress, and water parsley, and, climbing into the trees, the thorny white bryony vine. *Beware the white bryony,* her mother often said. The berries could kill, and just a bit of the root would empty your belly and void your bowels.

Grayling thought until she had a plan, which she told to Auld Nancy in a hiss and a whisper.

"What does Lord Mandrake want with you wenches?" the soldier asked. The firelight played on his features, illuminating small, dark eyes in a face marred with wounds old and new.

Grayling took a deep breath and said, "We are powerful witches. We, of all the witches in the world, possess the secret of invincibility, and he wants it."

"Nay," said the soldier. He picked at a sore on his

chin. "You are but an old woman and two girls. Tell me the truth."

Grayling caught Auld Nancy's eye across the fire and nodded. Auld Nancy nodded back. She rocked and murmured, crooned and shook her broom, and a sharp crack of thunder shook the ground.

The soldier jumped to his feet. "Fie upon it!" he shouted. "You *are* witches!" He sat and grabbed Pansy again. "*Invincibility,* you said. What means *invincibility?*"

"We have a potion that will make him powerful, immortal, and infinitely wise," Grayling said.

The soldier spat. "Nonsense. Then why are *you* not invincible?"

Grayling shook her head. "The potion does not work on witches. But one sip of our secret brew—"

"Make it for me."

"Nay. 'Tis too potent and special to give to just anyone."

Pansy gurgled again as the soldier's arm wrapped once more around her neck. "I am not just anyone," he said. "Do it."

"Let her go," Grayling said. "I would brew a draught for you, but I have no pot."

He loosened his hold on Pansy and kicked his iron helmet over to Grayling. "Now you do."

Trying not to smile, Grayling stood. She filled the helmet from the stream and placed it in the embers of the fire. She picked the herbs she needed — mint for its flavor and the gray, fleshy root of the white bryony for its power — and added them to the water when it boiled.

The soldier reached for it. "Nay," said Grayling, stopping his hand. "It must steep and cool a bit."

They sat in silence. Grayling chewed on a fingernail. *If this does not work, if his belly is out of sorts and that be all, we might wish we were back in the cage.*

"Now!" said the soldier. He reached for the helmet and sipped slowly. "Feh! 'Tis foul!"

"Invincibility is not easily won," Grayling said. "Drink it all. Pansy, come and sit here while the brew does its work."

There was quiet again, disturbed only by the sound of fighting some ways off. Auld Nancy, Pansy, and Grayling huddled together while the soldier nodded sleepily. Suddenly he jumped to his feet with a mighty groan. Grayling could hear his innards rumbling like thunder. "You!" he shouted as he lunged at her, but he was interrupted by the noisy spewing forth of the contents of his belly and his bowels.

"Run!" Grayling shouted.

The three raced along the stream, which ran stronger and faster as it flowed downhill. Grayling slipped in boggy patches, stumbled over tree roots, and snagged her skirts on thorny bushes. "Tangles and toadstones!" she muttered over and over.

A rickety bridge, made of reeds strung between lengths of rope, crossed over the stream. The span swayed, although no breeze stirred, and pieces of dried reed were sloughing off into the water. Grayling studied the bridge, the stream, and the terrain and shook her head. "We must cross to the other side to discover the grimoire's song again and return to the road west," she said, "but I misdoubt this creaky bridge can hold us." She threw some rocks onto the bridge to test for sturdiness and poked it with a tree branch. It shed more reeds but held.

Pansy shoved her aside. "Such dilly-dally! Bands of ruffians could be close after us. Let me by." She took a careful step onto the bridge, then another. It crackled and swayed but held. Another step, another step.

She looked back, grinned, and called, "'Tis sturdy eno —"

And with that, the bridge crumbled and dumped her in the water.

"Figs and fennel seeds," Grayling muttered. "This Pansy be more troublous than a stew pot full of snakes!" Taking Auld Nancy's broom, she scrambled down the bank to the stream.

She waded in near up to her knees and stretched the broom out to Pansy, who was floundering in the water, but instead of pulling Pansy out, Grayling found herself pulled in. She bounced and tumbled in the fast-running stream, while Auld Nancy scrambled alongside, calling, "Come back! Come back now!"

I would if I could, you foolish old woman, thought Grayling. *After I pushed Pansy to the very bottom!* Holding tight to Auld Nancy's broom, Grayling bumped on rocks, scraped on boulders, and tangled with tree branches as she was swept downstream. Swallowed water spewed from her mouth and her nose. Sodden skirts ensnarled her legs as she was thrown hither and thither through the surging stream.

A tangle of branches ahead promised a handhold.

Gulping and spitting, Grayling stretched to reach it, but the current spun her into a jumble of rocks. She knocked her head on the rocks again and again and felt dizzy with the pain, but finally, stone by stone, she dragged herself toward the bank while the churning water tried to pull her back. Finally she struggled out of the water and lay panting, lungs heaving, still clutching Auld Nancy's broom.

She was on the far side of the stream. Across the raging water, Pansy, who had also hauled herself out, stood with Auld Nancy. On the other side. The *wrong* side.

A plague on them both! thought Grayling. *Let them stay there. I will go elsewhere. Anywhere.* She was weary with leading and deciding, with child minding and old-woman tending. She would find some other way to rescue her mother.

She wrung what water she could from her cloak and her kirtle. Cursing and grumbling, she climbed up the bank toward the woods but slipped on the slippery soil and stumbled into an old oak, its bark pitted and thick and its branches gnarled. She could almost make out a face — its eyes closed and a knurl of bark like an open mouth. 'Twas not a tree but a man, his final screams hardened into bark. And beside him a sapling, a woman, hair fluttering with every breeze, tree up to her terrified eyes, unable to make a sound.

Filled with pity and horror, shaking with cold and wet and fear, Grayling stood there. The evil force had been here and was gone. Grayling was alone with what had been cunning folks, rooted to the ground, their limbs and hearts and brains trapped inside trees, bark and branches nearly to the tops of their heads. She could feel their terror and confusion. And this was true all through the kingdom — mages and wise women, people with skills and power, now wretched and defenseless. This undertaking, she realized, was not just a matter of freeing Hannah Strong but of freeing them all. And the only rescuers at hand were Auld Nancy, Pansy, and Grayling herself. She shook her head. She would not run. They might not win this fight, but she would not run.

She pushed her wet hair out of her face. Her first task was to sing to the grimoire and pray that, now she was on this side of the stream, it would hear her and sing back. And indeed it did. Her heart leaped. She slid back down the bank and waved to Auld Nancy.

"Come back, Grayling," Auld Nancy called.

"Nay! You must cross to this side of the water."

Shouting back and forth across the stream, they walked along the banks on both sides until they found a spot where the water ran less deep. A fallen tree lay halfway across.

"Hold on to the tree and cross," said Grayling. "Pansy, you help Auld Nancy."

Pansy shook her head, and her wet hair flew about her. "I will not go back into the water."

"Watch me," said Auld Nancy. "'Twill be easy." She waded into the water and grabbed for the tree. Hand over hand, she pulled herself along, her skirts swirling about her. Finally she was near enough so that Grayling could wade out and take her hand. The water came to their knees, and the strong current pulled them about. Auld Nancy fell and her hand was torn from Grayling's. For a moment Grayling thought the old woman would be swept downstream. She grabbed Auld Nancy by her skirt and held on. Together they staggered from the water and onto the bank, where they lay, breathing heavily and coughing up water.

"What about me?" Pansy called.

"Do as I did," Auld Nancy called back. "All but the falling."

"I cannot. I am afeared."

Muttering *"Fie! Fie! Fie!"* Grayling took her wet cloak off. She forced herself back into the water and paddled and pulled Pansy, mewling and whining, across.

Grayling wrung her skirt and her hair and emptied out her sodden shoes while Pansy wiped mud from her face with the hem of her kirtle. "You pigheaded, beef-witted noddypoop!" Grayling said. "This was all your doing. I should have just left you in the water at the beginning!"

"Do not waste breath, Grayling," said Auld Nancy. "Her mother did say Pansy was foolish." The old woman picked up her soggy broom. "Though it would be better for all of us, Pansy, if you were less so." Pansy thrust out her chin and narrowed her eyes but did not argue with Auld Nancy.

The old woman removed her wet cloak and shook it. Out fell a fish, which lay flapping on the ground. "Oooh!" Pansy said. "Make a fire, and we shall eat."

"No fire," said Grayling. She took the fish by the tail and tossed it back into the water. "We are still pursued by half the ruffians in the kingdom. Let us move on."

Damp and dripping, the three turned away from the stream and followed a path up to where it met the road.

Grayling could hear no sounds of fighting. She hoped the edge dwellers had been driven off, with the soldiers giving chase.

A sudden wind rose with a bite and a howl. It drove away the remains of the mist and swirled around the three travelers, clawing at their faces and tangling their skirts. Grayling's hair danced, and her eyes watered. Wet and clammy though she was, she shivered less from cold than from sudden feelings of dread, foreboding, and a terrible hopelessness. Then as abruptly as it had appeared, the wind subsided, the darkness lightened, and Grayling's spirits rose.

She grimaced. What kind of wind brings such darkling and despair? Shaking her head to clear it, she took Auld Nancy by the arm and continued on, Pansy panting and lagging behind.

"Where might Desdemona Cork be?" Grayling asked Auld Nancy after a time. "Will she find us again, or has she left us to continue without her?"

"When shall we rest?" asked Pansy. "I am fair spent. And when shall we eat?"

No one had answers. The way seemed to Grayling much longer afoot than it had in the back of a caged wagon, but at least they were not captives.

VIII

t last they reached the road west once more. There the setting sun illuminated a fantastical pavilion of marigold silk that flapped and fluttered in the breeze, making waves of golden cloth. At one side were a coach, paneled in green leather with brass fittings and scarlet window curtains, and a coachman asleep on the seat.

Before the pavilion stood a man. A very rich man, Grayling guessed, as she studied his velvet jacket, snow white breeches, and high-heeled black leather boots. He stood motionless, like a statue, like someone under a spell. A spell! Had the evil force been here? She took Auld Nancy and Pansy each by a hand, ready to flee.

Then from the pavilion came the aroma of roasting meat. And apple blossoms, out of season and unexpected, so all the more sweet. And lavender, mint, and rich honey.

Of course! Desdemona Cork! Grayling breathed out with relief. Desdemona Cork!

The lovely woman parted the silks and beckoned them in. Awestruck, Grayling looked about her. Draperies of crimson and indigo damask there were, and lavishly cushioned couches, beeswax candles and flaming torches, and small fires in bronze braziers warming the air.

While Grayling stood astounded, Pansy hobbled in and, with a great sigh, flopped onto a couch of ruby velvet. Auld Nancy, however, stopped at the entrance. "How come you by all this luxury?" she asked, frowning at Desdemona Cork. "You cannot be trusted, enchantress that you are. Who has given you all this to trap us?"

"Muzzle your tongue, grouching old crone," said Desdemona Cork. "The mayor of the town found himself besotted with me and furnished all you see. You and your ill temper are welcome to share it or not, as you choose."

Auld Nancy, bent with fatigue, shuffled in and dropped onto a cushion far from Desdemona Cork. Urged by Auld Nancy, Grayling, who still stood at the entry, related the story of their capture and escape. Pansy interrupted, saying, "Auld Nancy thinks Grayling was brave and a great help to us, which I could have been also, if I had wanted, but Grayling likes telling us what to do, so I let her do it." She snuffled loudly as she removed her boots and wiggled her dirty, blistered feet.

They all turned to look at Grayling. She blinked. Pansy had nearly gotten herself and Grayling drowned. Twice. Pansy whined and grumbled and complained at every turn. And she thought she could be brave and helpful? Grayling gritted her teeth. She had not wanted to lead, but who else was there?

"That is all over, and we have survived. Now I believe we must hurry away before we are discovered," she said, reluctantly, because of the warmth, the soft cushions, the aroma of the roast meat . . . and the still-missing Pook.

Auld Nancy, her face weariful and wan, said, "Desdemona Cork, be useful. Use your wiles to delay our pursuers for a time. Long enough for us to eat and to rest."

Desdemona Cork looked confused, as if the idea of being useful confounded her, but she nodded slowly. "You will be safe here until dawn. I can make it so." So Grayling, too, sat, choosing a cushion the green of the fiddlehead ferns in her valley.

Suddenly from outside the pavilion came the sounds of men shouting, the clanging of weapons, and the snorting of horses. The soldiers! Grayling jumped to her feet, her hunger gone.

Desdemona Cork stepped outside, and Grayling could smell roses. She moved closer to the entry and heard snatches of conversation. *Have you seen . . .* and *Whither the witches . . .* and *South. Due south, in a coach with four horses running fast.*

At a sudden shrieking, Grayling pulled back the silks and peered out. One of the soldiers was thrashing about, shouting and tugging at his clothes. Was he in the midst of a fit? Possessed of a demon? Out from a sleeve fell not a demon but a toad, brown and warty. Desdemona Cork squealed as it crawled over her foot and into the tent.

"Gray Eyes, this mouse has found you," said the toad to Grayling.

Grayling's chest swelled with joy. "Pook? 'Tis really you?" Although she much preferred Pook as a mouse or a raven or even a goat, she lifted Pook the toad and patted him gently on his bumpy back. "You are truly a remarkable creature to have found me," she said.

"I could not have walked such a far way, so this soldier carried me," said Pook the toad, "though he was unaware of his assistance."

"By my reckoning, you have now saved me twice," Grayling said, bowing her head. "My most grateful thanks to you and your mouse accomplices."

"Nay, the mice did what mice do: chew. 'Twas great fun for a mouse." Pook quivered, and Grayling, disinclined to put a toad in her pocket, held him gingerly on her palm.

After a few moments of shawl twitching and veil fluttering by Desdemona Cork, the soldiers, bowing and scraping, left, heading south as she had instructed them. The man in the high-heeled black leather boots still stood unmoving and unaware. Grayling gestured questioningly toward him.

"I grew tired of his attentions," said Desdemona Cork with a shrug.

Inside the pavilion, Desdemona Cork handed something to Grayling. It was her basket, left behind when the three were captured. She put Pook inside, where, in true toad fashion, he hid himself beneath the few remaining herbs, now limp and brown but welcome cover for a toad.

Grayling kicked off her soggy shoes, curled herself onto a soft cushion, and ate her fill of beef and apples and bread with honey. What a day she had had! Would she survive another like it? She combed her still-damp hair with her fingers and pulled it into a braid, then fell into a deep and dream-free sleep.

Dawn sun, shining through the silk, brightened the pavilion. The mist was gone. The travelers woke, comfortably rested and full of roast meat. "Now we must go," Grayling said. "I will sing to the grimoire, and we can follow."

Pansy stuck her blistered feet toward Grayling. "See you these? And my ankle is not yet mended. Can we not linger for a day or more?"

"And I," said Desdemona Cork, "I am weary—"

"Weary?" shouted Auld Nancy. "You, weary? I spent a night in a cage, crossed a river, and walked until my feet near fell off! And you think you are weary?"

"Me, I nearly drowned. Twice," said Pansy.

Auld Nancy shouted, "You are young and hardy. I am old and my—"

"Enough!" said Grayling, with surprising firmness. "I have seen such things as will haunt my dreams for years. Weary or no, I will go on—with you or alone. If there is a way to free all those who are rooted, I will find it. You do as you wish." She stood and wrapped her damp cloak, redolent with the stench of wet wool, about her.

"Fie, fie, you are most boasting and prideful today," said Pansy.

"Hush, Pansy," said Auld Nancy, climbing to her feet. "Of course I will go on. We will all go on." She crossed her arms and stared at Pansy and Desdemona Cork.

Pansy said, "I would not be left here alone." She frowned and pulled on her shoes.

Desdemona Cork huffed a lock of hair out of her face and reluctantly nodded. The company, now four once again, stepped outside.

The morning sky was blue and gold and the soft violet of woodland flowers. Grayling breathed deeply.

"As we continue west," said Desdemona Cork, "we

shall not encounter the soldiers, for I sent them else-where." She gestured toward the outside of the pavilion and the man standing there. "Sir Whoever-he-is will provide us with his coach and four. I will wake him."

"Nay. Such a splendid coach will attract unwelcome interest," said Grayling. "I would rather not meet the metal-nosed warlord or suchlike again."

"You, Desdemona Cork," said Auld Nancy as she waved her broom, "think ever of yourself. Grayling has the right of it. The coach would be too conspicuous."

"I say we take the coach for the sake of my poor feet," said Pansy.

Grayling bit her lip in consternation before asking Desdemona Cork, "What would happen when the enchantment wore off and he found us in his coach?"

Desdemona Cork frowned and sulked and twirled her skirts and her scarves. "If we cannot ride, I would prefer to return to the town and the mayor. You may go on without me."

"Still I will take the coach," Pansy insisted.

Auld Nancy turned on her. "You will do what I bid you!"

"Fie upon this company!" shouted Grayling. "Fie! I have had enough of the carping and scolding and bickering! Take the coach or do not take the coach. I am leaving!"

A sudden rumble of thunder shook the ground, followed by a flash of light. Grayling, Pansy, and Desdemona Cork all looked at Auld Nancy. "'Tweren't me," she said.

More thunder was followed by a swirl of smoke and the sound of trumpets. Grayling grabbed Auld Nancy's hand. Smoke and shadow! Were they discovered? Were they now doomed to be rooted to the ground?

I X

ut of the thick yellow smoke, a man appeared, a man as gnarled and knobby as a sack full of sticks. Charms and amulets, half hidden in his beard, clanked at his neck. "Who is it that disturbs the peace of the morning with squabbling?" His voice was between a rumble and a roar.

Auld Nancy stood and waved the smoke away from her face. "Sylvanus, be that you behind all the clamor?"

"Auld Nancy?" The booming voice was replaced by one more human and even elderly.

"Auld? Not so old compared to you. Except for

the food stains, your beard has gone quite white." Auld Nancy cackled. "I trust you are well. I have not seen you since the sad affair of the magic chickens."

"Sad indeed." The man's eyes filled with tears. "I was certain that a sprinkle of my flying powder would see those birds safely down from the roof. Alas, alas." His tears wet his cheeks and dampened his beard, and he wiped at them with a blue handkerchief. "Still, as the ancients say, 'tis better to try than to wonder.'"

Auld Nancy dismissed him with a wave. "This," she told the others, "be Sylvanus Vetch, adept of soothsaying, conjuration, and the casting of charms. He be teacher of enchanted scholarship at the school in Nether Finchbeck."

The school at Nether Finchbeck was a famed training academy for wizards, sorcerers, charmers, and spellbinders. *This unlikely looking magician must be powerful and important indeed,* thought Grayling. But if he were a famed magician, could he not have conjured a new cloak and better shoes? And why was he not rooted to the ground like so many others?

"These companions of mine," Auld Nancy continued, "are Desdemona Cork; Hannah Strong's daughter, Grayling; and the young Pansy, my niece Blanche's girl."

Desdemona Cork twitched her shawl, and Sylvanus looked at no one else. "An enchantress, I see," he said to her with an awkward bow. "And very . . . well, enchanting, I find." He waved his hand, and a large green bush near the path burst into bloom with creamy soft flowers. He slinked closer to her and presented her with a spice-scented bloom. "Sylvanus Vetch at your service, my lady — Brother Doctor Sylvanus Vetch, illustrious scholar, celebrated magician, and esteemed practitioner of tyromancy, or divination with cheese."

Desdemona Cork took the flower with a frown that was yet as lovely as any smile Grayling had seen, and Auld Nancy snorted. "Peace, Sylvanus! 'Tis not Desdemona Cork you should be attending but Grayling, who will tell you from the beginning what has befallen us."

And Grayling did. Her tongue was tired of telling the tale, and she was no closer to freeing Hannah Strong and the others than she had been at the start. But now Brother Doctor Sylvanus Vetch, who had called himself illustrious, celebrated, and esteemed, was here. Looking at the weepy, bony fellow gaping at Desdemona Cork, Grayling tried to bury her doubts. Perhaps their fortunes would change now for the better.

"Alas, alas," said Sylvanus when Grayling had

finished. He wiped his drippy eyes and nose on his sleeve. "To think the world is in such a state! I have heard rumors that the faculty of Nether Finchbeck is now a grove of hornbeam trees, grimoires and scrolls have been taken, and the students guzzle ale as they make vague and unsuitable rescue plans." Tears overflowed his eyes and disappeared into his beard until they emerged drop by drop at the bottom. "Alas, alas, oh, woe and sadness. 'Tis true that 'only the busy bee has no time for sorrow.'"

"Rumors? Only rumors? How did you not know, you who call yourself illustrious scholar and more?" Auld Nancy asked. "And how is it you, too, are not rooted to the ground?" She narrowed her eyes and peered at him.

He snuffled one last great snuffle and said, "Belike because I was not here. I was somewhere else. Somewhere" — he gestured vaguely toward the clouds — "else."

Grayling looked up to the sky but saw only sky.

Desdemona Cork asked, "Why have you, with the magic to make flowers bloom, not vanquished the evil force and made things right again?"

Pansy said, "Are you truly from Nether Finchbeck?"

Grayling broke in. "Do you, sir, have such a thing as a grimoire?"

With a great *harrumph,* Sylvanus said, "Nay, I have no need of a book for my spells. All my knowledge is stored here." He tapped his head with a bony finger.

"Likely that is why you have not been rooted," said Grayling.

Sylvanus smoothed his beard, smiled, and said, "Be of good cheer, fair mistresses. After hearing your sad tale, I shall favor you with my company for a time."

Company? Just *company?* "Can you do nothing to help?" Grayling asked him. "About the rooted folk and the grimoires, the smoke and shadow and the mysterious wind? Do you have no useful skills?"

The magician's eyes snapped. "I cannot combat the evil force until I know what it is," he said, "where it is from, why it was sent. That will take cogitation, consideration, contemplation, rumination. I cannot be hurried."

Grayling was not satisfied, but Sylvanus turned from her and whistled. A small spotted mule trotted out from between the trees. *Pook? Is it Pook? Is he now Pook the mule?* Grayling patted the herbs in her basket and was relieved to feel the shape of a sleeping toad. Nay, not Pook.

Sylvanus tightened the saddlebags that clanked against the mule's rough and dusty sides. "Shall we depart?"

Grayling, Auld Nancy, Desdemona Cork, and Pansy looked at each other, at Sylvanus, and then back at each other. Finally Auld Nancy shrugged and nodded.

As Sylvanus started to climb onto the mule, Grayling pulled on his tunic. "Do you not think," she asked in a soft voice, "Auld Nancy might ride? Her bones pain her something fierce."

"Nay," said Auld Nancy, with a shake of her head. "Better for the beast to carry Pansy. She is most pale and frail-looking of a sudden, though I cannot think why."

Pansy was to ride? Grayling thought that would be excellent, if only Pansy would ride elsewhere. Away. Anywhere but there.

"Foolish coddling," said Sylvanus, grabbing the mule's lead. "The girl is young enough to be strong and hardy. As they say, 'a new shoe lasts longer than an old.' Why, in my day, we not only did not ride mules, we sometimes carried them on our shoulders, for animals were precious and to be cared for, whereas we teemed with young people." He combed his beard thoughtfully with his fingers. "I remember once when I had two beasts to pack over the Hermantine Pass in winter—"

"Enough," Auld Nancy said, and she shook her

broom at him. "Enough talk from you. Hailstones and thunder clouds! I don't know if you have more words or more tears, but they both try my patience."

Sylvanus scowled while Pansy climbed onto the mule. "What be in here?" Pansy asked, poking the saddlebags. "They do be lumpy and uncomfortable under a rider."

"Leave off my belongings, wretched girl," said Sylvanus, and he swatted her hands away. Pansy snorted and settled onto the mule's back.

Auld Nancy was right, Grayling thought. Pansy definitely ailed. She'd lost her rosy plumpness. Her eyes were ringed with shadows, and she hadn't whined or mentioned food in minutes.

As they left, Grayling turned to take a last look at the flowers Sylvanus had conjured. The bush was black and blighted, the lovely blooms shriveled. "Magic always has a price," said Auld Nancy.

Grayling turned away, took a deep breath, and once more sang to her grimoire. The grimoire sang back. "Hurry. This way," she said to her companions, and they followed her, heading away from the sunrise — west, the grimoire sang them ever west.

Their steps grew slower as the morning wore on, and now and then one of them stopped to rub one sore body part or another. Every sound made Grayling startle and look around, but other travelers were few and none seemed apt to threaten them.

By late morning, the sun had dried her cloak a bit, but the sun beat fiercely on the back of her neck. She envied Auld Nancy the protection of her wimple. Finally she unloosed her braid and let her hair hang down her back to cover and cool her.

On and on they walked, on and on. The morning turned to bright afternoon, and the sun shone in Grayling's face. She had no hair there to let down. Maybe she could grow her eyebrows long enough to cover her. She snorted at the image and slowed down to walk next to Auld Nancy. "You can command the rain," she said to the old woman. "Can you then make clouds to cover the sun? My face is sizzling like a sausage in a fry pan."

Auld Nancy shook her head. "Belike any magic will call attention to us."

Grayling thought of the warlord. She nodded. But without using her magic, Auld Nancy had no more power than Grayling.

After a time, Auld Nancy and Sylvanus lagged

behind, each with a hand on the mule for support, and Grayling found herself walking beside Desdemona Cork. She sniffed deeply of the scent of roses. "I have been wondering," she said to the lovely woman. "How is it to have people admire you and obey you and seek to satisfy your every wish?"

Desdemona Cork pushed her cloud of hair back from her face. "'Tis useful at times, and often amusing, but very wearying. And when the enchantment wears off, folks are confused, and I am abandoned." She sighed a sigh that sounded like a spring breeze ruffling the meadow grass. "If I could choose, I would live in a cottage by the sea, make fresh bread, spin in the sunshine, and live on goat cheese and apples." She sighed again. "Alone. Blessedly alone and untroubled by the wishes of others."

"Could you not choose to live so now?" asked Grayling.

Desdemona Cork smiled, and a faint rose color tinged her cheeks. "I suppose I could. A cottage by the sea . . ." She fell into a thoughtful silence.

In such circumstances, Grayling wondered, *would I choose the cottage over such magic as Desdemona Cork's?* The word *cottage* awakened memories of rain on the roof thatch, the comforting whisper of her mother's spinning wheel, and mugs of warm cabbage soup. Soup. Her belly rumbled. Desdemona Cork's roast meat seemed so long ago. When might they eat again? And what? Would they be reduced to catching and cooking weasels and badgers?

"I have gone my limit," Auld Nancy said at last, while the sun still shone in the sky, "and can walk no more now, not with these old bones." She sat on a stump and rubbed her knees, and Sylvanus dropped down beside her. Pansy slid off the mule's back and stretched. Grayling could not say who looked the more weary.

She put her basket down, and Pook the toad crawled out. He flipped his pink tongue at a passing insect, snatched it right out of the air, and gulped it down. Then with a shudder, he became Pook the mouse again. "This mouse is grateful for this new shifting," he said, "for he feels much disgust at the eating of bugs." He spat a tiny spit before clambering up Grayling's skirts and into her pocket. Grayling peered into the basket with its cargo of blackened herbs, bits of broken jars, and toad droppings. With a homesick sigh, she dropped it at the side of the road.

She turned to Auld Nancy and, at the sight of her drooping there, frowned with concern. Auld Nancy had been less peevish of late, Grayling realized, and less bossy, as if she did not have the strength. Pain marked the old woman's face as she rubbed her neck and her knees.

Grayling bent down to Sylvanus. "Is there aught you can do to relieve Auld Nancy?"

The magician shook his head.

"Not spell? Charm? Incantation?" Grayling grew increasingly frustrated with him. "Not draught? Elixir? Brew? Anything?"

Sylvanus waved her away. "I choose not to deplete my skills by using them on petty complaints."

Grayling scowled at his selfishness and dropped down next to Auld Nancy. "I have heard my mother sing a song," she said to the old woman, "that might help with your pains." She began to chant, slowly and softly:

> *Aches from cold,*
> *Aches from old,*
> *Aches, go away.*
> *Rub rocks and stones,*
> *And not old bones.*
> *Aches, go away.*
> *Let Nancy rest,*
> *Not feel so old.*
> *Aches, go away.*

After a few moments, Auld Nancy stretched her limbs and smiled. "I believe that did help some. Almost like magic. Gramercy, Grayling."

"You would do better to thank Hannah Strong, for it be her song."

"Aye," Auld Nancy said, "but 'twas your voice and your goodwill."

When they were ready for the road once more, Sylvanus helped Auld Nancy onto the mule. Pansy, of course, sulked. Grayling reflected that Pansy was irritating, annoying, and a hindrance on this journey. Why hadn't Auld Nancy sent her back to her mother? Her mother was a reader of palms. Perhaps she had a grimoire and enough magic to be rooted, too? Was that why Pansy was here?

No matter the why. Pansy *was* here and walking next to Grayling. "When did you come to Auld Nancy?" Grayling asked.

"'Twas shortly after Lammas Day. My mother sent me to make something of myself."

"Were you not something already?"

"Not something my mother approves. For the most part, she looks at me and sighs."

"I know that sigh," said Grayling, shaking her head.

"Feeble Wits, my mother calls me, and Pigeon Liver. Are you now becoming something?" she asked Pansy. "Has your time with Auld Nancy changed you? Are you—"

Pansy interrupted. "I hope we will be eating soon."

Seemingly not, then, Grayling thought.

"We turn here," Sylvanus called, and he led the mule onto a rutted path that headed due south.

"Nay," Grayling said. She gestured to the west. "The grimoire is this way."

"We must first call on the widow Bagley, whose cottage is through here. She has a cinnamon and garlic cheese I must sample. Certes, the struggle between the two strong essences will provoke especially powerful visions."

While Grayling stuttered "but . . . but . . . but . . ." and pointed west, Desdemona Cork, stumbling over a tree root on the rough and rugged path, asked, "Cheese? We are doing this for cheese?"

"Aye. As you know, I am an adept of divination with cheese."

"I thought that was a silly jest," said Grayling as she joined the others on the path to the cheese woman's cottage.

Sylvanus scowled at her. "Many things," he said,

"have the power to foretell the future or discover what is hidden. Not only cheese but dust, flour, roosters, and ice, if you know how to use them."

"Nay," said Grayling.

"Aye," said Sylvanus. "Also spiders, pig bladders, and shoes."

"Truly?" asked Grayling.

"Truly," said Sylvanus.

Grayling shook her head. The world outside her valley was full of wondrous things, but was the wonder worth the trouble?

X

he path narrowed, and wild black-
berry bushes on either side reached out
to snag Grayling's hair and her skirt. Soon it curved to
reveal a clearing and Widow Bagley's home. The dwelling was more hut than cottage, and the thatched roof was
quickly becoming unthatched. In the yard sheep, goats,
and a red cow grazed while tubs and tuns and a big vat
bubbled unattended. The cottage door was open — or
missing — and from inside came the odor of sour milk
and herbs.

An old woman appeared and beckoned them in. *By pig and pie*, thought Grayling, *she is even older than Auld Nancy, if that be possible*. Desdemona Cork waved the invitation away, Pansy turned away, and Auld Nancy nodded on the mule's back, but Grayling, curious, followed Sylvanus.

The cottage was dark and damp, and its sharp, musty smell made her nose burn. Dripping bundles of drying cheese hung from the roof over the table, making puddles that a yellow cat was lapping. Wax-covered orbs of finished cheese were hung in the rafters to smoke and in dark corners to age. The room looked to Grayling like a magical forest where cheese grew instead of flowers.

Sylvanus approached the cheeses. He rolled his eyes and twitched his nose, sniffing and poking and tasting slices of the creamy rounds. "This," he said finally to Widow Bagley. "This cheese I will have, and I will give you two coppers for two rounds."

Widow Bagley snorted. "Six coppers," she said.

Sylvanus shook his head. "Six? Nonsense. 'Tis thievery and greediness. I will give three."

"Eight coppers," said the widow.

"Eight? Nay. 'Tis not done that way. When I increase

my offer, you lower your price until we meet in the middle. Four, and that be my last offer."

"Twelve," said the widow.

Sylvanus sputtered. "You do not understand bargaining. I increase, and you decrease. Now I offer six, and 'tis absolutely as high as I will go. What say you?"

"Done!" said the widow, and she spit on her hand and offered it to Sylvanus.

Sylvanus cheerfully paid the amount she had demanded in the first place and left the cottage with two cheeses tied together and hung around his neck. The others hurried behind him. *He is obviously no shrewd bargainer*, Grayling thought, *and he believes in magic cheese.* Was he but a muddle-headed dolt and no help to them at all?

They turned again to the west, Pansy shuffling in the rear. Amidst the trees, the remains of a cottage still smoked. And there, as if standing guard, was a tall tree, not human anymore but not quite tree. Grayling poked Sylvanus with her elbow and bade him look. His face, what she could see of it beyond the beard, paled. *Why had he not seen such before? Where had he been?*

A fierce and menacing wind blew against them, buffeting them as they struggled against it, heads down. The wind bit at Grayling's chin, clutched at her ankles, and crawled up the sleeves of her gown. Her heart grew cold, and she felt dark despair settling over her spirits again as she trudged on. Suddenly, with a last swirl of dust, the wind was gone.

Nor was this a natural wind, Grayling sensed. Something was happening, something ominous and bleak, something they could not understand or control. Would it only strengthen as they drew closer to the grimoires? How could they fight it? She looked at her ragtag band of companions, muttering and grumbling and limping, and she succumbed for the moment to the despair.

"How much longer must we trudge this road?" asked Desdemona Cork. "I wish to be quit of the journey."

Grayling sang a snatch of song and cocked her head to listen. "The grimoire is near," she said. "Mayhap we will reach it next day or the next."

Auld Nancy scowled. "I fear this be too easily done—"

"Easy? You think this easy?" Grayling's cheeks blazed. "I have left my mother rooted to the ground, trekked through woods and swamps, been threatened and menaced and imprisoned, suffered blisters, frights, and empty belly. I do not in any way think this easy!"

"Hist, girl. I did not mean 'twas not difficult, for all of us, but I wonder why some power would take the grimoires and then let us find them."

"Easy?" Grayling muttered as she plowed on. "She says 'easy'?"

The day was darkening when they stopped again, feet sore and bellies empty. Pansy huddled beneath a tree, her face gray with weariness, and Auld Nancy dropped down beside her.

Trees stood black against the sky, and all was silent but for the hoots of owls and shrieks of birds for which Grayling had no name. The very air seemed dark and heavy. Though reluctant to be alone among the trees, Grayling went to gather wood for a fire.

A bit of a brook, muddy and stagnant, seeped from ground rutted and tunneled by moles and voles. She glimpsed foxes and furry creatures she hoped were not wolves darting between the trees. Every rustle of leaf or crack of twig underfoot made her jump. Branches reached for her like fingers groping, poking, scratching. Had some of these trees been folks, were perhaps still folks deep in their woody hearts? At last, her arms full of branches and twigs, she hurried back to the others.

Sylvanus was sitting with his back against the rough

bark of a sweet chestnut tree, his eyes closed, his shoulders festooned with autumn leaves. Pansy was whispering to Auld Nancy and Desdemona Cork, and they looked up at Grayling.

Pansy motioned to her. Grayling dropped the wood and joined the others. "We are wondering over Sylvanus," Pansy said.

"Why has he not turned tree," asked Auld Nancy, "or even seen the damage? He heard rumors, he said. What has he been busy doing?"

"Was it something with smoke and shadow?" Desdemona Cork asked in a whisper.

Pansy cleared her throat and said, "I have a worrisome uneasiness about what he carries in his saddlebags. Belike we should examine them."

The four turned and studied Sylvanus. His eyes were still closed, and he whistled, puffed, and snorted, every breath ruffling his beard. He did not look so very sly or treacherous to Grayling, but then she had little knowledge of treachery.

"Sylvanus," said Auld Nancy, kicking his foot. "Wake, Sylvanus. We would speak with you."

Sylvanus stretched and shook his head. "I was not asleep but merely thinking about the problems of the universe. Very difficult work it is, thinking deep thoughts, and 'the mind cannot grapple when the body is weary.'"

Auld Nancy kicked his foot again. "Fie, you old braggart. Stop your *thinking* for a moment. We would see what you carry in those saddlebags."

"Ah, woe, what is it that causes you to distrust me? I have always done my best." He snuffled. "But 'tis true, 'no man is a hero to those who wash his socks,' as the eminent professor Isidore Muchnick once told me."

"Enough!" cried Auld Nancy. "Enough! You ever grizzle and yawl! I swear someone has put a babbling spell on you. Pansy, fetch the bags. We shall see for ourselves if he has been about mischief."

Pansy lifted the saddlebags and shook them. Out fell a blue velvet cap and cape, copper coins, a clean shirt, two metal cups with strange engravings, bottles of various green and slimy things, brown bread, two onions, and a ham.

"Ham!" Auld Nancy shouted. "Ham! You did not tell us you had food! Let us forget this discord for a moment and eat."

Pansy grinned a sly, satisfied grin. She had known about the ham in Sylvanus's bags, Grayling was certain of it. But how?

Sylvanus stood. "Are you convinced I carry nothing suspicious in my bags? Leave me now to soothe my stomach and my nerves and put my bodily humors back in balance." He grabbed his velvet cap from Pansy. "And cease pawing my things, you great, useless lump of a girl!"

Pansy's grin faded, replaced by her usual sullen pout.

After Sylvanus stowed his things back in his saddlebags, Auld Nancy said, "I will slice ham. Sylvanus, start us a fire."

Grayling watched him with interest. The man was a magician. Would he snap his fingers to start the fire? Or gesture? Point? Clap his hands?

Sylvanus pulled a tinderbox from a pocket of his dust-colored gown. He saw Grayling's disappointed face and shrugged.

"What would suit that ham, Sylvanus," said Desdemona Cork, and the scent of almond blossoms filled the air, "is a bit of that cheese hanging around your neck."

Sylvanus threw an arm protectively across his chest and shook his head. "'Tis not cheese for eating. It has a purpose."

"Beyond filling our bellies, I take it," said Auld Nancy.

A nearby shrub offered late sweet whortleberries, and with the ham and an onion from Sylvanus's saddlebags, they had a fine supper even without the cheese. Grayling dropped a bit of berry into her pocket for Pook, but the mouse said, "Nay, I fear my belly still suffers from the toad's dinners." With a burp, he snuggled deeper.

While they ate, the company aired their various worries and concerns, for which none of them had answers. They all spoke at once: "How much farther? Why the wind? Will we find the grimoire? What else is in store for us?"

"You, Graybeard," Auld Nancy said to Sylvanus. "Help us. Ask your cheese what it knows."

He shook his head and held the cheeses close to his chest.

"Is that not its purpose?" Auld Nancy asked. "Why we called at the widow's cottage? Show us how it is done."

With what might have been a groan or a grumble or a growl, Sylvanus removed the cheeses from around his neck. With his knife he sliced small bits from each round and dropped them into the smaller of his metal cups, which he placed on the embers of the fire while muttering strange mutters and chanting peculiar chants.

The melting cheese gave off the aroma of sour milk

and cinnamon, and Grayling, though full of berries and ham, thought they might do better to eat the cheese than do whatever Sylvanus was planning.

"You, girl," he said finally to Pansy, "fetch water." He held the larger cup out to her.

Pansy limped and moaned so as she edged closer to him that Grayling snatched the cup herself. She found her way back to the muddy brook and returned with a cup of water.

Sylvanus's chants grew louder as he took the cup with the cheese from the fire, protecting his hand with the hem of his gown, and poured its contents into the larger cup in a stream, making loops and coils on the surface of the water. There was a sizzle as the hot cheese met the cold water, and then silence.

Sylvanus poured the cooled cheese onto the ground. "The shape the cheese has taken will tell us what we need to know," he said.

"It looks like a lump of cheese," Grayling said.

Sylvanus frowned at her. "I must concentrate," he said, and he studied the cheese from all directions. He broke off small bits, rubbed and smelled them. "Indeed," he said finally, "a lump of cheese."

"What means that?" asked Grayling. "Does it tell us who is behind this evil smoke and shadow?"

"It tells us it is a lump of cheese! A lump of cheese!" Sylvanus shouted. "The cheese is useless."

"Do not fret, Sylvanus," said Auld Nancy, patting his arm. "Leastwise, now we can eat it." She used Sylvanus's knife to cut a large section from the rounds of cheese for each of them. Then, their bellies full and their lips still blue from berries, they lay beneath the trees on beds of fallen leaves and fern fronds. All was silent but for Sylvanus now and then muttering, "Lump of cheese!"

Grayling felt Pook leave her pocket to feast on the seeds and crumbs of cheese on the ground. Satisfied, he groomed his whiskers and, with a sigh, crawled over her skirt and settled in her pocket once more. She smiled. What little time it had taken for her to become attached to him. A mouse! At home she would have chased him from the cottage with a broom and a curse. But here . . . she patted her pocket tenderly before she fell asleep.

In the morning, Grayling sang her way forward, and the others followed. The woods here were different from the woods in Grayling's valley. The air was damper, the ground wetter. Ancient moss-laden oaks rose from thick carpets of ferns, and willow branches, laden still with mist, trailed nearly to the ground like the long sleeves of a wedding dress. Downed trees supported young sprouts whose roots arched around the logs, seeking the ground. "Nurse logs," said Sylvanus. "They give life and support to the young trees."

"In truth?" Grayling asked him.

"In truth."

"And there truly is such a thing as soothsaying with cheese?"

"Most certainly," said Sylvanus.

"The world is full of things most peculiar," she said.

"And things most astounding, young Grayling. Most astounding. Why, in places in this world are snails so big folks can live in their shells."

"No!"

Sylvanus nodded so heartily that crumbs of cheese flew from his beard. "Aye. And to the west are islands where men have the heads of hounds and go naked in all types of weather. And another where people have horses' feet. Would you not like to see these places?"

"No, I want only to go home," Grayling said at once. But men with horses' feet? That she would like to see.

From time to time the wind blew through, icy and sharp, and then subsided, leaving the air thick and heavy. Grayling found breathing difficult. Her lungs hurt from the effort and her steps grew slower and slower, but she sang on as she walked.

As they ventured farther, there was no path, and Grayling lurched and stumbled as she forced her way through, tearing her bodice and scraping her arms on the thorny bushes. Auld Nancy and Desdemona Cork followed, but Sylvanus and Pansy hung back, jostling to be last in line, snarling at each other like two ill-tempered but cowardly dogs.

They pushed through to a sort of clearing, foreboding and dark with dread. Here the trees were thinner and blackened, the ground scorched as if by fire. Charred wood and ashes crunched beneath their feet. Even Sylvanus's spotted mule was ill at ease. Eyes round with fear and nose speckled with foam, he began to back away, and Sylvanus had to urge, wheedle, and pull him forward.

Grayling heard the sound of something moving just beyond, something large, moving slowly, smoothly over the ground. The air was dense with the smell of smoke, scorched wood, and something unidentifiable—acrid and sharp and bitter in the nose. Then came a gibbering and groaning, a howling and hissing, from nowhere and everywhere, reverberating. Grayling covered her ears, but the sound was inside her, pounding and echoing.

She grabbed Auld Nancy's hand and stood as if frozen, and her companions lurched into her. Gliding toward them was a horrid creature, all scales and flames and teeth.

X I

huge snake, big enough to swallow a man whole, slithered into the clearing. Its black scaled body, rippling and throbbing, coiled around itself. Its eyes flamed red, and, opening its huge mouth, the snake hissed and howled and breathed fire.

Flames turned trees into torches and sizzled as they met patches of mist and dew. There came a great fluttering in Grayling's pocket, and Pook burst forth, a raven again. With a harsh *cronk,* a *squawk,* and a flapping of wings, he soared into the sky and away. The mule made a sound between a whinny and a grunt and, ears flattened, bolted, saddlebags swinging.

The snake flicked its tail and coiled it around Grayling, pulling her close and squeezing her breathless. A harsh odor burned her throat and stung her eyes. She struggled to breathe. Twisting and wriggling, she fought to free herself, but the snake held her tight. She could do nothing.

Pansy and Desdemona Cork had run away, but Grayling could see Sylvanus, rubbing his beard and mumbling incantations, and Auld Nancy, poking the snake's middle with her broom and screeching, over and over.

Whether it was due to Sylvanus's magical intervention or Auld Nancy's battering, Grayling did not know or care, but the snake opened its mouth, flicked its sharp tongue, and loosed its coils.

Bruised and sore, reeking of the serpent's stink, trembling with terror, Grayling turned and ran with Sylvanus and Auld Nancy back into the thicket of trees, where they caught up with Pansy and Desdemona Cork.

Together they tore out from the trees onto a path that twisted and turned on its way back to the road. Finally, when they heard nothing behind them but the whooshing sound of fire and the crack of branches snapping from the heat, they stumbled to a stop. Grayling doubled over, trying to catch her breath. Her face smarted and her legs trembled. Auld Nancy dropped to the ground, her head drooping. Pansy pulled at the old woman's sleeve, bleating, "We must go! Up! Up!"

Although Grayling too was eager to put distance between herself and the monstrous snake, she knew Auld Nancy did not have the strength to rise and run farther. And the day was growing dark. They could not see to flee or to hide. Desdemona Cork helped Grayling gather enough fallen leaves and bracken to make a bed, and hungry and cold and frightened, the five travelers huddled together like kittens.

It was dawn when Grayling woke to Sylvanus saying, "'Tis important to note that the serpent has not followed nor threatened us."

"Certes, those flames were a threat," said Desdemona Cork, her face gray beneath her blue markings. She stood, brushing leaves from her veils and shawls and skirts. "'Tis foolish to put ourselves in such danger. I am away."

Auld Nancy said, "Desdemona Cork! You cannot think to be on the road alone, not with the smoke and shadow on one side and that terrible creature on the other. 'Twould not be safe. We must stay together."

"And do what?" Desdemona Cork asked. She looked up the road and down. Grayling could see the pulse pounding in the enchantress's throat. Shaking her hair and her skirts, Desdemona Cork sat down again, and Auld Nancy took her hand.

"Now, Sylvanus," said Auld Nancy, "what meant you?"

"I mean, I believe the beast is there but to keep us from the grimoires. We will come to no harm unless we try to get closer."

I was in the snake's grasp, Grayling thought. *Certes, I felt that the creature meant me harm, and I have bruises to prove it.* She shivered at the recollection. "We are here because the grimoires may tell us what to do about the evil force," she said. "And my mother's grimoire is through those woods. We *must* get closer." Her legs ached, and her head hurt, and she wished to be anywhere else. "But how can we ever get past such a creature?"

"Alas, we cannot," said Sylvanus in a voice hollow and forlorn. "Best we leave it for some master magician to come and—"

"I thought *you* were a master magician, Sylvanus," said Auld Nancy. "The others are rooted to the ground. There must be something you can do."

"Nay," said Sylvanus, blowing his nose. "Alas, alas, I cannot."

"My mother and all the others," said Grayling, "are we just to leave them spellbound? Let them turn completely into trees? What will happen to the world if all the witches and wizards and cunning folk are helpless, and all the power rests in the evil force?" She rubbed her ash-smudged face with her sleeve. "You say you know charms and conjuration. What use is your enchanted scholarship if you can do nothing?"

Said Sylvanus, "Wise men say, 'when your foe breathes fire, 'tis folly to be brave.'"

A brisk wind set tall trees to groaning, dead leaves swirled around Grayling's feet, and the cries of foxes and badgers echoed through the woods. Pansy clung to Auld Nancy's skirts, and no one made a sound but for the thumping of their hearts.

Grayling was afraid. She studied the others. Sylvanus Vetch, teacher of enchanted scholarship at the school in Nether Finchbeck, he, too, was afraid. Auld Nancy with her bluster, skittish Desdemona Cork, fainthearted Pansy, and Grayling herself—all afraid.

Grayling cast about for some way to embolden them. What would Hannah Strong do? "My mother," Grayling said at last, "has a heartening song, and I believe we are in need of one now." And she sang loud and sweet and true:

> *You cannot just sit here,*
> *Dreaming and hoping.*
> *March forward to battle*
> *With pennants unfurled.*
> *I call on your courage,*
> *No fretting or moping.*
> *Stand tall.*
> *Stand tall.*
>
> *If we stand alone,*
> *It still must be done.*
> *If it must be done,*
> *You are the one.*

"*And you, and you, and you,*" she sang, gesturing to each of her companions. *And me*, Grayling thought, with a shudder. *And me.*

The words of the song settled softly on their hearts like snowflakes, and they were cheered. "Enough fussing and dawdling," said Auld Nancy, clapping her hands. "I shall attack this creature with thunder and lightning and send him scuttling in fear like a lamb fleeing a wolf!" She stood, smoothed her skirts and her wimple, and turned back the way they had come. "If I do not set myself afire first."

The others stumbled behind her, down the road, over the blackened ground, and through the charred and shriveled trees. They approached the clearing with steps that grew slower and slower.

While the others took cover behind a tree, Auld Nancy stepped forward. "Hie, snake," she shouted in a shaky voice. She cleared her throat and began again. "Hie, are you here? Show yourself!" There was no response, and she turned with a shrug to the others.

And then, with a cracking of branches and crunching of bushes, the snake slipped into the clearing. Grayling vowed she could hear a heart pounding wildly in every chest, even the serpent's.

The great snake opened its mouth, hissed and howled, and spit flames. Grayling heard the whoosh of the flames, the crackle of branches afire, and the *cronk* of a raven, as Pook — she thought it must be Pook — tore through the blazing branches and soared into the sky, his tail feathers aflame.

Auld Nancy backed up a few steps, lifted her broom, and began to chant:

> *O spirits of the storm,*
> *Let fire meet earth.*
> *Let a storm spring forth*
> *And shafts of fire come down*
> *To assault our enemy and strike him low.*
> *So might it be.*

She muttered and murmured, swaying with her eyes closed and broom pointing to the sky.

> *May my power bring lightning,*
> *May my anger bring thunder.*
> *Open, skies, and rend clouds asunder!*

Suddenly the sky turned dark and thunder cracked. Lightning split the air and splintered trees, bringing branches crashing to the ground. Sparks flared and sizzled, scorching Sylvanus's gown and Pansy's hair. Flashes of lightning lit the clearing; thunder rumbled and roared.

Grayling had pulled her cloak over her head and did not peek out until the commotion had ended. She was grieved to see the snake still there, massive and scaly and untouched by Auld Nancy's lightning. It coiled its quivering body, switched its tail, and let loose a ghastly hiss.

The company fled back into the woods. At a safe distance, Auld Nancy, face red and hands atremble, dropped to the ground. "I cannot direct the lightning truly enough to strike the beast, and I know nothing more to do."

Grayling felt her face sag like an empty feed sack. She turned to Desdemona Cork, but the enchantress shook her head. "I have had no practice enchanting monstrous serpents, nor do I wish to learn. I say we go elsewhere."

"Sylvanus," said Auld Nancy, with Pansy hiding behind her skirts, "I challenged the creature, and, though scorched, I still stand. Might you not try?"

Sylvanus's face paled with fear, but Grayling took his hand and squeezed gently. Pulling his cloak tightly about him, he moved again toward the clearing, the others trailing far behind. He narrowed his eyes and glowered at the creature, which blew fire. Grayling near choked in the ash-and-cinder-filled air.

Sylvanus hastened back toward the trees where the others waited. "'Tis well known," he said, "that a true magician casts spells and curses at a distance. Preferably a great, great distance."

He said *ahh* and *hmm* several times, scratched his nose, and rubbed his beard. He peeked from behind a tree and stared at the serpent for long moments. He muttered and swayed, cleared his throat, and hummed. He lifted a pine branch still smoldering and shook it in the beast's direction. "Foul creature from the depths of the earth, beast of fire and doom, may you vanish, retreat, exist no more," he intoned.

Grayling peered around Sylvanus. The snake was still there.

With another shake of the fiery branch, Sylvanus called, "May you become as small as a drop of rain, a grain of sand, a hummingbird's eye, the elbow of a flea. May you become so small you become nothing at all, and trouble us no more."

The snake still was there. Its serpentine body quivered and sparks flew from its mouth.

Sylvanus rubbed his nose and rumpled his hair.

"That was my finest dematerializing spell. Defeating monsters is not my expertise, I fear. I can do no more."

His magic was as useless as Auld Nancy's. Grayling's belly clenched like a fist. Had the serpent defeated them? Was their journey over? *No,* she told herself. *No!*

Grayling studied the snake carefully. "Sylvanus, look. 'Tis odd, but the creature has changed some." She went a little closer. "I can almost see through it, as if it were made of a fine, thin cloth with something moving behind, a shape here, a shadow there."

Sylvanus looked. "Aye, 'tis strange." He studied the beast. "I expect that this creature is not a serpent at all but a glamour, and my spell has caused the glamour to thin." Grayling shook her head in puzzlement, so Sylvanus continued. "There be three kinds of serpents: serpents by nature, serpents by spell or curse, and serpents by glamour. A magic spell turns a person *into* a serpent. A glamour spell makes a person appear to be a serpent, but in truth he is not. 'Tis but an illusion."

An illusion? The coils squeezing her had felt very real. "Can a glamour spell be overturned?"

"Someone must be brave and determined enough to reach a hand through the glamour and grasp the one bewitched through the beastly guise."

"Be you certain, Sylvanus?" asked Auld Nancy. "It sounds too easy."

"Easy, you say again? *Easy?*" Grayling spit and sputtered. "Easy for you, perhaps, who does not have to put her hand through a scaly, hissing creature." For Grayling knew it must be she. She had grown fond of her companions—well, not Pansy—but did not think any of them brave and determined enough to approach the monstrous serpent. Was she? Could she risk the snake's crushing grasp again?

Her heart was racing and her palms sweaty, and although she wanted only to run away, she went a little closer and looked up, up, up.

The serpent opened its mouth and flicked its tongue but spat no fire.

Breathing heavily, Grayling stepped closer, and closer yet. Slowly she reached out a trembling hand and touched it. She felt the leathery scales, the muscles beneath, but then her hand passed right through and met the solid, warm flesh of a hand grasping hers. Startled, she jumped back.

The very air quivered, and the ground shook. A great hiss rose from the creature, which twisted and thrashed.

Flames blistered her nose and singed her hair. A shower of ashes, another deafening hiss, and the snake disappeared. And there in its place stood a boy—nay, a young man, strong of arms and shoulders but pale, as if he had spent his life indoors, with hair and eyes of honey brown, and a smile, thought Grayling, bright enough to warm a winter night.

Grayling fell back, her mouth agape, and her companions cried out in dismay. Who was this fellow? Was this another sort of glamour that made a hideous serpent appear to be a pleasant-looking young man so it could get close enough to crush them?

"I am relieved to be released but confused and stupid with not knowing what has befallen me," the fellow said. "Shall I thank you, fair mistress, for freeing me from this monstrous guise, or was it you who cursed me at the start?"

"Nay," Grayling answered, "not I. We but came upon you. I must confess I much prefer you in this condition. Who are you?"

"Phinaeus Moon," he said with a small bow, "apprentice paper maker from Wooten Magna, at the end of the Great Stony Road." He gestured past the trees. "Returning from delivering a load of paper to the stationers' guild in Lesser Beamish, my bladder was so overburdened I stopped to let my water go. A great noise came, and I felt the earth shake and a voice thundered, 'Be you now guardian of my house and all that is in it. Let no one pass or you shall be serpent evermore.'"

The company was struck dumb, all but Pansy, who moved to the young man's side. "That was impressive, was it not?" she said with a smug smile. "I did labor long to word the spell just right."

XII

pell?" Sylvanus spluttered. "You, you useless lump of a girl, have been meddling in magic?"

"Urk," said Pansy. And then, "Urk!" The girl was trembling with rage. "Do not call me a lump! Or useless! I can . . . I could tell you . . . I have done . . ." She stopped. Her eyes were dark and cold, and she clenched her lips together.

"Pansy, child," Auld Nancy asked, "what have you been playing at?"

Pansy backed away. Her face was ashen, but her cheeks flamed. "I am not a child, and I am not playing!" she shouted. "I have more power than you thought I did. I played the fool and you laughed at me, but I have surprised you, have I not? You did not know I had such skills. My mother did not know. But harken to me: I took your grimoires and rooted your cunning folk. I placed a glamour spell on this boy to guard the grimoires. You never suspected me, but I did it. Me!" She put her hands on her hips and smirked in triumph.

There was such silence that Grayling could hear her heart beating and the anxious twitching of Desdemona Cork's skirts. Her belly grew hot with anger.

Finally Auld Nancy darted forward and grabbed Pansy's arm. "Why, Pansy? Why have you done this?"

"I wanted to know what you others know, so I took the grimoires to learn. And I planted the cunning folk." She shrugged. "I did not want to kill them, but prevent them following me."

Auld Nancy scowled and said, "Spiteful, careless girl. You do not deserve the power you have."

"My power, I found, has limits." Pansy shook her head. "I conjured the force that comes as smoke and shadow, but it has grown ever more powerful, larger and fiercer and harder to control. I did not know what it would do next, or to whom, and feared I might be in danger. You seemed to have a plan, so I struggled to keep the force away, although it wearied and sickened me. I wanted you to succeed so I would be safe."

"Why was I spared? And Sylvanus and Desdemona Cork?" Auld Nancy asked.

"You? All of you with no grimoires, no real magic, and little power? I did not bother with you, thinking you no threat."

Sylvanus spluttered again, but Auld Nancy waved him silent. "Where did you learn such spells? Your mother never taught you to be so selfish and careless," she said.

"How soon," asked Grayling, her voice tight with fury, "can you undo the damage you have caused?"

"And," added Phinaeus, "retrieve my horse and wagon?"

They all looked at Pansy, who shook her head. "I can do nothing. 'Tis grown too strong, overwhelming my spells, taking the grimoires and guarding them fiercely. 'Tis a mighty force now, and I am empty and drained and so tired." She took a long, shuddering breath, and her lips trembled. "We may all be planted ere long."

Sylvanus scowled at her. "You forgot the third rule of magic: *Do no magic you cannot undo.*"

Auld Nancy grabbed Pansy by an ear. "Stupid, greedy, malicious girl! I will shake you until your bones turn to butter!" She shook the girl roughly. "Then I shall send you back to your mother and tell her what you have done." Another shake. "That you are thoughtless and dangerous and a disgrace to your family." And another. "That you should be sent to be dung heap tender or assistant pig keeper."

"Huzzah!" Sylvanus broke in with a shout. "Huzzah! I have but now realized—the cheese was not useless. The lump of cheese pointed to this lump of a girl. I just did not understand. Yes, yes, I knew it! 'Tis a true soothsaying cheese!" His face fell into disappointed folds. "But now we have eaten it, and it is gone! Alas, alas. True soothsaying cheese, and we have eaten it!"

As Grayling watched and listened, the heat of anger rose from her belly to her face. Her hands itched to thump Pansy until she bellowed. Certain that thumping Pansy would not help, for they might yet need her goodwill, Grayling closed her eyes and breathed deeply, soothing herself with thoughts of moonlight, lavender wands, and sorrel soup with dumplings.

From somewhere behind them came an unearthly sound, a sound between a bellow and a bawl, a sound of menace and pain and despair. Grayling held her breath, prepared to face another snake.

Sylvanus shouted, "Nostradamus!" and ran toward the sound. What was that magic word he shouted? she wondered. And why hadn't he tried it on the serpent?

A rustling in the trees startled her, and she turned to see. The branches parted, and there was Sylvanus and . . . his mule!

"Nostradamus did not run far," said Sylvanus, beaming at the mule, "and now he is with us again."

Only his mule! Grayling shook her head to clear it. The snake, the smoke and shadow, Pansy's confession — they had left her most jittery.

Now that the clearing was serpent free, Grayling gathered wood, and Sylvanus built a fire; Desdemona Cork sat beside Auld Nancy and gently rubbed the old woman's aching knees; Phinaeus Moon studied them all in bemusement. Pansy came to sit among them, but the others turned their backs, and she slunk off to sulk alone.

When the fire was blazing, the company warmed their toes as they emptied the saddlebags that had returned with Nostradamus and ate the remains of the ham, bread, and onions.

Grayling jumped to her feet, shuddering. Some vermin was crawling up her arm! Spider? Rat? Flea? "'Tis this Pook, Gray Eyes," said a small voice. And there he was, pink nose, and pink ears, and more whiskers than any mouse truly needed. "Has that horrid creature gone?" He twitched his tail, charred at the end where the flames had found the raven.

"Aye," Grayling said, "truly gone, and you are come back safely." She settled back down by the fire, and the mouse curled against her neck.

"This Pook should not have abandoned you, but it is difficult for a startled raven to stay in a pocket." Pook twitched his nose. "Might there be a crumb of something to eat?" Grayling gave him a bit of bread, which he nibbled before climbing into her pocket. She heard a tiny sigh and then a tiny snore.

"Was that mouse talking?" asked Phinaeus Moon, his voice quavering with alarm, suspicion, disbelief.

Grayling had forgotten that he was newly come. "Aye, he was," she said.

"A mouse? But how?"

Grayling told again the story of the mouse and the potions. "And now whenever he be fearful or excited, the shape shifting takes him. He finds it thrilling, he says, but confusing."

Phinaeus Moon stared at her. His mouth hung open, and his eyes were wide as dinner plates. "Who are you folk?" he asked at last. "A lady of surpassing loveliness, a mischief-making girl with powerful magic, a weather charmer, a bearded wizard, a talking mouse, and you with the courage to face a hideous serpent?"

So Grayling had to begin from the very beginning, with her mother calling to her. He listened and nodded until she finished.

Sylvanus lit a pipe, and Grayling smelled dried mint, sage, and angelica root. "Until you, I had not met someone glamoured to be a snake," Sylvanus told the young man. "Could you feel it happening? Did you know how you appeared to others?"

"I felt little different. A bit queasy and dizzy perhaps, as if I had overdrunk of honey mead, but little different except that I moved as if through soup, a thick and warm soup—my granny's dried pea with bacon perhaps." Phinaeus Moon licked his lips at the memory.

"Even my horse bellowed in fright and ran, the cart bouncing after him, and my companions fled. I looked into a stream and saw, oh, how very different I was. I wished I could run from me also." He shivered. "I am no beauty, I know, but to be horrid, repulsive . . . and all thanks to this meddlesome, irksome girl." He glowered at Pansy.

She glowered back at him. "I could likely cast a glamour again," she said, "so I suggest you stop calling me names."

"Pansy was cruel and malicious," said Auld Nancy. "We will teach her to use her skills wisely, Sylvanus and I, or she will be put to work in the Nether Finchbeck laundry, washing the socks of adolescent magicians."

Said Sylvanus, "The second most important rule about magic is to know when not to use it. We shall attend to that anon."

Pansy frowned.

The fire took to smoldering and smoking, and Auld Nancy coughed deeply as the smoke circled her head. "Black clouds and ashweed, begone from me!" she shouted, waving her broom. A small shower of rain fell and cleaned the air. She sat back, satisfied.

Grayling stirred the fire and added small twigs and branches. The fire settled down, and so did they all.

"I don't suppose," asked Phinaeus Moon, "any of you could conjure me a horse? I must get back to the city." He looked around. No horse appeared. "No, I feared not. 'Tis afoot for me."

"What awaits you in the city?" asked Auld Nancy. "A banker? A tailor? A lover?"

"Paper," he said. "Fine paper that I make myself." He stretched his hands out before him. "My hands tingle, longing to feel again the slippery rag slurry that dries into paper. That, too, is a sort of magic. My paper is unequaled in the kingdom—heavy, soft, creamy, and thick." His eyes grew dreamy. "Paper not to be used for registers or accounts or lists of provisions: *two pounds of flour, a tub of pig fat, and a turnip.* No, elegant paper that should be saved for royal decrees, sacred texts, or"— here he looked at Desdemona Cork—"love letters."

Desdemona Cork twitched her shawl, and Phinaeus Moon blushed.

Grayling rolled her eyes. "Can you not leave it for a moment?" she hissed to Desdemona Cork. "Must you enchant everyone?"

Desdemona Cork pulled her shawls tightly around her. "'Tis not something I do, but something I am."

"Why, then, are you not something useful?" Grayling asked. "Why are none of you useful? What value is there in your magic if you can do nothing with it?" She roared in frustration. Where was the help she had expected from the *others?*

Sylvanus snapped his fingers, and spring flowers bloomed on the branches of autumn-brown shrubs. A rainbow appeared in the darkening sky, and tiny winged creatures flew by. Grayling looked closely. Lambs. They were tiny winged lambs.

Useless! No wonder they had not been rooted like the others! Even Pansy had thought them not worth the effort. Anger formed a sour knot in her throat as she curled up to sleep.

"I have heard the grimoire again. 'Tis just past there," Grayling said next morning. She gestured to where the woods were thick with great green spruces and firs, bare-branched rowans and oaks, packed tightly together, tangled with ferns and brambles and briers.

Her body taut with apprehension, Grayling led the others farther into the woods. The power that Pansy had conjured, the power that now defied her, would it be destroyed or destroyer? Grayling felt suddenly chilled.

After a time, she stopped at a break in the trees. Up a rugged, bracken-frosted rise was a great stone house, towered and turreted and spired as if trying to touch the sky.

"My mother's grimoire is inside," Grayling said. "Mayhap all the grimoires are there. Since the serpent is now but a bumbling boy and no longer guarding them, they are unprotected. Could not someone fetch my mother's grimoire?"

There was silence but for Phinaeus Moon's muttered "*Bumbling?* How say you *bumbling?*"

"I hear no one proposing to go after it." Grayling sniffed. "Should not perilous adventures have a hero to face any dangers?"

The women looked at Sylvanus and Phinaeus Moon, who looked at each other. No one spoke.

I have been the most wary and unwilling of us all, thought Grayling. *How did I become leader?* But she was. She sang, and the grimoire sang back. "'Tis in there indeed. With my mother's grimoire, mayhap we can discover how to end this bother at last."

"In truth," said Pansy, "there are no answers or

assistance in your mother's grimoire or anyone's. There has not been such a force before, so there will be no remedies in a grimoire's pages. I knew this when we began to follow your grimoire's song, but I didn't want you to stop trying, because I didn't know what else to do."

Auld Nancy, Desdemona Cork, Sylvanus, Phinaeus Moon all were struck dumb, but Grayling, her temper as frayed as her skirts, shouted, "All this for nothing? This exhausting journey for nothing? When we might well have stayed warm and dry and fed and sought another solution? Pansy, you are worse than malicious. You are wicked! A very devil!"

"I preferred you when you were timid and quiet," said Pansy.

"Muzzle up!" said Grayling. "This all be your fault."

"Why is she still here?" asked Desdemona Cork, pointing at Pansy. "Why do we not send her away?"

"I have promised my niece to watch over her girl and keep her safe," said Auld Nancy. She shook her head. "It appears that the only danger to Pansy may be from herself. Still, though I have promised, we need not keep company with the girl."

"I am here," said Pansy. "Talk to me, not about me."

"Do I hear a gnat buzzing?" asked Desdemona Cork.

"Clod-pated fools," Pansy said in a mumble, and she stalked away.

"Pansy may be useful yet," Auld Nancy said, "and she cannot do too much harm while we're watching her."

"If what Pansy said is true," asked Grayling, "and there are no answers in the grimoires, what, then, shall we do? Auld Nancy? Desdemona Cork? Sylvanus, master magician?"

All shook their heads. Weary and disheartened, they sat, leaning against the trees. Grayling stormed away, disturbing Pook, who, jolted out of her pocket, landed a goat.

Somewhere near was the sea. Grayling could hear it and smell it. She knew the sea only from songs and stories, but she could see it in her mind, gray and vast and wild, surging and churning. That was just how she felt. Such turmoil within her. She could swallow it no longer. She followed the sound through a thicket of young oaks and over a rise.

And there it was, not as she had imagined it but wilder and fiercer, more magnificent and more immense. The waves racing in put her in mind of great frothy beasts attacking the shore, over and over, in endless battle. The wind, a clean wind with no trace of smoke or shadow, blew through her hair, lifted it, and danced it furiously upon her head.

As her exhilaration turned to rage, she let out a great howl: all this way and all these days and all their efforts, and still they were powerless against the smoke and shadow. Shadow and smoke. Smoke. Smoke . . . She paced many moments in thought before heading back to the others.

Pook the goat bleated at her return, twigs sticking out between his large yellow teeth. Auld Nancy, Desdemona Cork, and Sylvanus were sprawled on the ground. But where was Phinaeus Moon? Perhaps he had already gone, back to the city. *Well, indeed,* Grayling thought, *we have no need of him, good for nothing but gawking at Desdemona Cork.*

She cleared her throat and said, "Do you recall Auld Nancy clearing the smoke away from her with a small rain shower?" Her companions nodded. "I do wonder, if a little wet rid us of a little smoke, might not a lot of wet extinguish a lot of smoke?"

There was silence as her listeners struggled to understand just what she meant, and then "Aha!" from Auld

Nancy. "Indeed," she went on, lifting her broom, "I shall call up rain."

Sylvanus stroked his beard. "The girl may have the right of it, but rain would likely be too scant. To banish the demon of smoke and shadow would require a great deal of water and no way to avoid it."

"I was thinking," said Grayling, "of the sea."

"The sea, the sea," the others murmured as they looked at her and each other.

"We have followed my mother's grimoire all this way," said Grayling. "The force was summoned to gather the grimoires and guard them. Although Pansy's gatekeeper has been removed, the force must guard them still. If we find some way to take my mother's grimoire, will the force not follow to retrieve it, as it was created to do?" The others looked at each other and bobbed their heads in agreement. "We could then throw the grimoire into the sea. The smoke will pursue it and be extinguished. Might that be an answer?"

"It might," said Auld Nancy, "but 'twould be most dangersome."

"No matter. I, Phinaeus Moon, shall find the grimoire for you and hurl it into the sea," said the young man, returning with a load of wood in his arms. "I would be the hero of this adventure."

Grayling shook her head. "Nay. You cannot sing to the grimoire nor hear it singing back." She looked at frail Auld Nancy with her aching bones, sweetly scented Desdemona Cork with her frivolous enchantments, and white-bearded, wise, but ineffectual Sylvanus. Though they each had a portion of magic, the grimoire would sing to none of them. Only to Grayling. Only to her.

"I fear it must be me," she said.

As Phinaeus Moon started a fire, the others nodded somberly. *Who else indeed. I must,* she repeated to herself, *I must,* though every part of her wanted to run, to hide, to disappear. Instead she curled herself near the fire and tried to sleep. A biting-cold wind arose from time to time, but whether it was natural or a sign that the force was protesting her plans, Grayling could not say.

XIII

rayling watched the sky lighten from murky dawn to the bright blue of a fine autumn day. The sky should not be blue this morning, she thought, but cloudy, dark, and ominous.

She stirred the embers of the fire and sat beside it, reluctant to face what was to come. One by one, the others woke, stood, and stretched, until only Desdemona Cork still lay on the ground, curled around herself like a puppy.

She raised her head. "I am sore afraid," she said. "For myself, for Grayling, for us all. This is nothing I can enchant away." Auld Nancy dropped creakily down beside Desdemona Cork and took her hand.

"What if she does not succeed?" Desdemona Cork asked. "What if we all are rooted? I can almost feel my skin harden into bark." She shuddered.

It proved the seriousness of their plight, thought Grayling—the bold and bossy Auld Nancy, who mistrusted enchanters, bringing a measure of comfort to Desdemona Cork, no longer arrogant and assured but doubtful and in need of solace.

Grayling inhaled deeply. She would do what she could—for her mother, for the other rooted folk, for all those in peril. Taking the sleeping Pook, once more a mouse, from her pocket, she asked, "Will one of you safeguard Pook while I am occupied?"

Phinaeus Moon, with a small smile, reached for the mouse. Pook, however, would have none of it. "Nay, mistress," he said with a squeak, "this mouse shall go with you."

"Ah, you are still compelled by the binding potion," said Grayling. "Perhaps Sylvanus can counteract it."

"Mistress Gray Eyes," said Pook, "in truth the binding potion wore off long ago, but still this mouse will go with you." He clambered up to Grayling's shoulder and settled himself against her neck with a soft *huff*.

Grayling's heart grew warm. Mice were not known for their loyalty, but here was Pook, facing danger with her and for her. *Loyal as a mouse, that's what people should say.*

Sylvanus muttered some words over Grayling and sprinkled her with mint leaves to bring good fortune. Auld Nancy struggled to her feet, joints cracking and creaking. "Have a care, child," she said as she smoothed Grayling's hair and her skirts. "See you don't trip as you run, and come right back if the deed seems too fearsome."

Pansy bid Grayling no farewell nor wished her well. She but watched silently from behind a tree.

Grayling climbed through the bracken and up the rise. She heard a howling in the distance that set the back of her neck a-prickle. Was it wolves? The sea? The wind? None of those betokened anything good for her. She climbed on, her heart beating frantically.

The day grew cold and sunless, and the wind began again to blow. It howled and bit and bellowed. Dried leaves crackled and scurried along the ground, and seabirds screeched like wild-haired hags about the fire on

All Hallow's Eve. Tall evergreens bent so far that their branches swept the ground. The very earth shook.

A blast of wind like a massive hand pushed Grayling back. Her hair tangled, and her skirts swirled. She stumbled and fell. Righting herself with some effort, she bent into the tempest and followed the path until the house loomed right before her, its walls streaked with moss and darkened by damp.

A tall wooden door, hanging from rusted hinges, banged in the wind. It whined on its hinges as she pushed it wider. Inside, it was dark and dank, for the high, narrow window slits let in little light. The very stones in the wall, slimy with the damp of centuries, exuded cold. She could feel the chill right through the thin and tattered soles of her shoes, and her breath spun clouds.

Grayling shivered but not just at the iciness. Evil chilled her like the frost of a winter night. Her belly cramped with fear and revulsion. "What is it I feel? Is the force here?" she asked aloud, her voice echoing in the emptiness. She stroked Pook softly to comfort him — or maybe herself. "Might you, my Pook, shift into something huge and menacing to frighten it away?"

"You well know, Gray Eyes, that this mouse cannot choose the time or manner of the shifting," Pook said. "But a mouse is good at scampering and sleuthing unseen. Put this mouse down, and it shall see what is here." She dropped him gently down, and he ran off, slipping on the slick stones of the floor.

Grayling wrapped her arms about herself to stop her shivering. The room seemed large but empty, of people, of furniture, of life. She called *whoo hoo, whoo hoo* to hear it echo but stopped with a gulp. "Blast, but I am a goose," she said in a frightened whisper, "making it so easy for me to be discovered."

Taking a deep breath, she sang to the grimoire and, hearing it sing back, smiled in relief for a moment. The grimoire was indeed here, and it knew her.

Away from the entry hall, the darkness was so deep that she had to feel her way through the house. The walls were damp and sticky, and she stopped often to wipe her hands on her skirt. Through doorway here, step up here and down there, hallway here, blank wall there, she moved slowly, following the grimoire's song.

One dark, cold room followed another. Grayling grew dizzy with the turns and turnabouts. From somewhere behind her came the moaning of wind gathering, and a sudden blast of icy air slammed her against a wall. Grayling struggled to flee as the wind battered her face and sucked out her very breath. "Why don't you just root me like the others," Grayling shouted in defiance, "or leave me alone!" She ducked and shoved her way through, but where was she? The air grew yet colder and darker, and she tripped and fell over something.

Books. Many books. She examined them in the dim light from a slit window high in the wall. Grimoires! Grimoires higgledy-piggledy, here and there. Grimoires in tottering stacks, big and small, some thick with pages, some as thin as a maple leaf, silk covered and leather covered and bound between rough skins. *There must be near a hundred,* Grayling thought. She never knew there were so many cunning folk in the kingdom.

With the *tick tick*ing of little nails, Pook skittered to a stop.

"'Tis the grimoires, Pook!"

"This mouse does not know what is a grimoire."

"'Tis a book of spells and songs and recipes."

Pook shook his soft gray head. "This mouse sees only piles of paper marred with ink and not good for eating."

"You silly mouse, that is just what we were looking for." But something evil had settled on the grimoires like dust, and she was loath to touch them further. Likely the evil force would fight to retrieve any grimoire she took. Should she take the time to search for her mother's or simply lay hands on the nearest one?

Nay, she thought, *who knows what curse or protective spell has been laid on another's grimoire. I must find our own.* She sang, as clear and strong as she could, and the air above the grimoires shivered and glistened. Grayling listened carefully. "'Tis here," she said, with a small smile of relief. And she sang again. "Here." She plucked a book from the pile and recognized it as her mother's, the faded blue cover marked with a burdock leaf in a circle. As she pulled it toward her, she felt the chill of a shadow behind her. No time, no time!

"Pook! Go back to the others! Go back!" She ran through the house, twisting and turning. She feared she would never find her way out again. Finally she glimpsed light from the open door, and she hurried out. Lightning flashed here and there. Thunder shook the ground. Where was the path to the sea?

She burst through a holly thicket behind the house and there below was the sea, enormous, powerful, even monstrous. The crashing of the waves was like armies meeting. She held the grimoire to her as she raced helter-skelter, followed by the thrumming of a force, churning up smoke and shadow, heat and ice, freezing branches and shrubs, scorching her kirtle and her hair. Her breath came fast as she tripped and stumbled down the steep and treacherous path, over the pebbly shore, and onto wet and slippery rocks that reached out into the water. The sea was so vast, and she was so afraid.

Smoke and shadow howled up the path behind her. Her eyes and nose filled with smoke. Icy hands clutched her face, her neck, holding her, pulling her back. Enveloped in dark and cold, Grayling was overtaken by despair. She could not escape. It was over. But still, smoke and shadow behind and above and all around her, she made one last effort and plunged into the sea, into the water, which closed over her.

XIV

he seawater was bitter cold, salty on her lips, and stinging in her eyes. After her plunge to the bottom, she drifted there, quiet, at ease. Was she dead? The water was above her and around her, embracing her, enfolding her, cradling her. It was so lovely, so peaceful, until her chest tightened and her lungs began to burn. Which way was up? Which way was air? She paddled wildly. Her skirts billowed and snagged her legs, and her hair tangled in her eyes and her mouth.

Her struggles took her at last to the surface, where

she gulped great gulps of air. The seawater she had swallowed roiled in her belly and spewed out like a fountain. No, she was not dead. She felt too miserable to be dead. She closed her eyes and bobbed gently in the water while a seabird screeched above her.

A sudden splash near her proved to be Phinaeus Moon, who had hurled himself off the rocks. He caught and held her.

"Let me go," she shouted, batting at his arm. "You are pulling my hair."

"Stop fighting and let me help. I am rescuing you."

"Nay, let me rescue myself."

They staggered to the beach, where they lay wet and gasping. "Fie and fie again, Grayling!" said Phinaeus Moon. "You were supposed to throw the book into the water, not follow it in."

"I had no choice. The smoke and shadow and I, we were one, tangled together and not separable." She shuddered, feeling once more the foul cloud, icy and afire at the same time, that had enveloped her.

The bird continued its screeching, accompanied by frenzied shouting from the cliff above. Grayling lifted her head to see. There were Auld Nancy and Sylvanus calling and waving and bouncing with glee. Desdemona

Cork, wrapped in her fluttering shawls, pointed to the sky and cried, "Look there, look!"

Grayling looked. A great stream of birds poured from the rise where the stone house was. Birds of different sizes, different colors, strange birds, with no beaks or wings . . . Nay, not birds! Books! "Phinaeus Moon, 'tis the grimoires!" Grayling cried. And it was — large grimoires and small, old and new, artfully wrought and plain, more than a hundred grimoires sailing through the air and on. "What does it mean?"

Phinaeus Moon stood and craned his neck to see better. "Belike they are flying back to their owners!" He clapped his hands and laughed. "I think you have done it! Grayling, you have broken the spell!"

A smile lighted Grayling's face as joy rose within her. "And their owners? Might this mean they too are released?"

With a shrug Phinaeus Moon said, "I am not the person to ask. Perhaps Auld Nancy could say. Or Pansy." He took Grayling by the arm. "Come, I'll help you back up. Certes, you will allow me that."

Grayling, queasy, tattered, and wet but lighter of heart, nodded, and Phinaeus Moon led her up a steep but straight path to where the others waited.

Auld Nancy, twittering in a most un-Auld-Nancy-like way, grabbed Grayling's arm and held her close. Sylvanus and Desdemona Cork danced delightedly. Pansy stood alone at the edge of the group and glowered.

"Here, come warm yourself, girl," said Sylvanus at last, clucking with concern as he pulled Grayling closer to a welcoming fire. Desdemona Cork removed Grayling's sodden cloak and wrapped her in a shawl of fine wool woven in stripes of gold and the silvery blue of the sea. It had a sweet, exotic spicy smell — spring flowers and fresh apples with a touch of cinnamon and — Grayling buried her face in it — warm wine on a cold night. She breathed deeply.

They gathered about the fire, Grayling safe and warm between Desdemona Cork and Auld Nancy. "Is the force gone now?" Grayling asked, when she had settled herself. "Is the horror over and all as it was before? Are my mother and all the wise folk released?"

"By meddling in magic," said Sylvanus, "Pansy opened a door, and evil has come through. There may be more surprises in store, but for the moment, I would say the trouble is over."

Phinaeus Moon came and crouched near Grayling. He took a drenched and dripping book from beneath his doublet. "I saw this sinking as I jumped into the water, and I was able to take hold of it." Grayling reached for the sodden grimoire. "Soft, soft," he said, holding it away. "The pages are soaked and fragile, and the ink is smeared in places." He placed the book in Grayling's lap.

She opened the grimoire and for the first time saw inside. Here was a recipe for her mother's rosehip jelly, there the ingredients for a love potion. Grayling examined page after page: a chant to find lost sheep, songs for healing and comforting and cheering, careful drawings of the leaves of deadly nightshade and monkshood root. Grayling had learned much of this lore by watching and listening to her mother. What Pansy had wanted to know so desperately that she conjured the smoke and shadow was not in these pages. There was no sorcery, no mysterious secret, no magic here.

"If you please," Phinaeus Moon continued, "I will take it and repair it." He took it gently into his big hands. "Most pages need only to dry. The others I will have recopied on my good paper. Creamy, thick paper, smooth to the touch but strong and altogether splendid" — he smiled at her — "just as you are."

Grayling smiled back as she studied him — his eyes warm and deep, hair a soft brown. The very air around him seemed to shimmer. "Oh, figs and feathers, he's an enchanter!" she whispered, and shook her head violently to break the spell.

"Nay," said Desdemona Cork. "He is but an ordinary young man. 'Tis his gentle kindness that shines."

Grayling gawked at Desdemona Cork. "I thought you did not notice us ordinary folk."

Said Desdemona Cork, "I am learning."

The scream of a seabird interrupted. Was it Pook? Grayling wondered. Or was he still a mouse? Had he come back as she ordered him? If not, where was he? And *what* was he? It was difficult keeping track of a creature that changed its nature so frequently.

Grayling looked at Pansy, across the fire. Firelight made shadows on Pansy's face, which was not stupid and sullen as usual, but sly and malevolent. Had she done something else wicked?

Pook! If she had hurt Pook, Grayling would . . . would . . . what would she do? It would be something severe and horrid.

"Where is Pook?" Grayling asked.

"I am here," said the mouse as he scrabbled up her arm. "'Twas a long way for a mouse to come. I hurried as fast as I could, but my legs are short and my heart is little. Now I am here, and you are safe." With a contented huff, he climbed into Grayling's pocket, damp though it was, and settled in for a well-earned rest.

Weary and hungry, the company dozed by the fire. When Grayling woke, the sun was setting over the sea, splashing streaks of pale oranges and golds and a tinge of lavender across the sky where it met the horizon. The air was rich with the smell of salt and seaweed. Phinaeus Moon had gathered clams and mussels and periwinkles from the shore. Sylvanus pried open the shells with his knife, Desdemona Cork rinsed them in seawater, and Auld Nancy wrapped them in sea lettuce and cooked them briefly on the hot coals. Grayling gathered berries and wild celery. It was not much of a supper for six, for they let Pansy share, but it did taste good.

"We must leave here," Sylvanus said through a mouthful of berries. "We must see whether our deeds have truly broken the spell and what damage has been done."

"What if nothing has changed?" asked Grayling. "What if the grimoires have flown off, but people are still rooted? What if the force did not dissipate in the sea but is still there, and Pansy cannot call it back, nor can you?"

Sylvanus wiped his mouth with his beard. "Soft, girl, soft. Don't fall off the cliff until you get to the edge. We shall see what we shall see."

That is the worry, thought Grayling. *What* shall *we see?*

In the morning, Phinaeus Moon bade them farewell. He would be going north along the seashore while the others walked east, back the way they had come. "How will I recover the grimoire?" Grayling asked him.

"Sing to it, and follow. It will be waiting." With a wink, a grin, and a whistle, he was off, headed north.

Grayling watched him go, her heart suddenly sore. Soon the others would be leaving her also. She was at last free to see about her mother, but she could not imagine her days without them.

Stumbling and limping, the remaining travelers pushed through the woods, up hills and down, over ditches and fallen logs, until they came to a road. The walking was easier then, and the company had gone some ways when a small open carriage with a noble crest on the door came up behind them on the road. Desdemona Cork tossed her hair and twitched her shawls, and the carriage stopped.

"What about your cottage by the sea?" Grayling asked, grabbing Desdemona Cork's arm. "Goat cheese and apples? Remember? You can stop enchanting and bake bread." She untangled a leaf of wild celery that was stuck in the enchantress's cloud of hair.

"I am what I am," said Desdemona Cork. She flashed Grayling a smile of rare loveliness, and Grayling felt again the pull of the woman's power.

Grayling unwrapped the gold and blue shawl from around her shoulders and handed it to Desdemona Cork.

"Nay, keep it," said Desdemona Cork. "Think on me from time to time, wind in my hair, spinning by the sea. No matter that I will not be there." She climbed into the carriage, which continued on its way, blowing a great dust storm up in its wake.

Those left behind coughed and rubbed their eyes. Auld Nancy, angry, lifted her broom. "We shall see how enchanting she be with rain in her face!"

Grayling took her hand. "Your rain, like your anger, Auld Nancy, will fall on all of us."

Auld Nancy grumbled but put her broom down.

Two were gone now. Grayling would never smell sweet blossoms or feel soft sun on her face without thinking of Desdemona Cork.

They began again to walk, away from the sea, away from their adventures, toward home.

Pansy dawdled behind the rest and whined. "Sylvanus, I want to ride the mule. My feet are blistered and sore tired, and my head hurts."

"If you hadn't wearied yourself with devilment, you would not be tired out now," Sylvanus called to her. Pansy opened her mouth to speak, but Sylvanus silenced her with a wave of his hand. "I will not burden him. Nostradamus has a far way to go to Nether Finchbeck."

Pansy dragged and shuffled her feet but finally caught up with the others. "Tell me more of this place," she said to Sylvanus.

"Nether Finchbeck?" His eyes unfocused, as if he were looking far into the distance and back into the past at the same. "Nether Finchbeck. A glorious institution of learning and spelling and necromancing, where mystery and manifestations of brilliance share the day with sheer befuddlement."

"I long to be a powerful magician," said Pansy. "Take me with you."

"Nay, never," said Sylvanus, shaking his head. "Or leastwise, not now. You have much to learn before you can be considered for Nether Finchbeck. You will go with Auld Nancy for the learning of it."

"Nay," said Pansy.

Sylvanus frowned at her. "'Twill be worth the effort, girl, to achieve mastery, and power, and a thoughtful nature. After all, 'an empty head makes noise but no sense.'"

Pansy was silent, though her face was stormy.

The day was cold but sunny. Thin clouds made pictures in the sky and then passed on. Grayling and Auld Nancy now lagged behind the other two, for Auld Nancy's weary bones slowed her down and Grayling was loath to leave the old woman's side. Folks passed to and fro on the road, often gawking at the four bedraggled strangers with the mule, but none stopped to engage them. Had any of them been rooted to the ground and then set free? Grayling wondered. Or were the trees at the roadside more than they seemed?

Long past noon, they reached a crossroads. "We part ways here," Sylvanus said. "I must make certain the evil has passed and all is as it was before."

Pansy grabbed Sylvanus's sleeve. "Take me with you! I have skills. You have seen them. Teach me to do great magic."

Sylvanus pulled his arm away. "Nay, I said. I have seen your skills overcome by emotions you could not control. Your envy, greed, and anger burst forth in the power of the smoke and shadow, and you endangered us all. Auld Nancy has much to teach you."

"I do not want to learn. I want to do!"

"And that is the primary reason you go with Auld Nancy." Pansy's face crumpled. "And, you," Sylvanus said to Grayling, "you have proved yourself clever and brave."

"Nay, I was most fearful, for I knew I had no magic to help me."

Sylvanus whistled to his mule. "Only the very stupid do not fear danger," he said. "And as for magic, the great wizard Gastronomus Bing of happy memory said true magic is like a sausage."

Auld Nancy and Pansy listened intently, while Grayling's jaw dropped in befuddlement. "Sausage? How sausage?"

"Made of bits and pieces of things everyone has— not pork and spices but tricks and charms, aptitudes and powers, some herbs, some skill and training, and some luck." He tightened the straps of the saddlebags on the mule, and Nostradamus grunted. "The world is full of mystery. Not everything can be explained. Does that make it magic? You could sing to the grimoire with no words and no music and hear it singing back. How? Was this magic? Was it in you? In the song? Or does it speak of a bond between you and the grimoire?" Sylvanus pushed a wisp of hair from Grayling's face. "And there is magic of sorts in your courage and your keen wits, the songs you called upon, and your caring heart."

Grayling sniffed. Whatever skills she had were not at all awesome and astounding, not what she would call magical. She could not command smoke and shadow or shroud a boy in a glamour spell as Pansy had. But Pansy's magic just caused trouble. Did magic always bring trouble? Would having magic be worth being as irritating and vexatious as Pansy?

"How was it, Sylvanus," Grayling asked him, "that you knew nothing of the smoke and shadow and the damage it caused when we found you?"

"I was elsewhere, traveling," said Sylvanus, "partaking of the pure aether there beyond the moon . . ."

Grayling ruckled her forehead in suspicion.

"Aye, you have the right of it. In truth," he said, "I knew of the smoke and shadow, and I had concluded that the force's magic was so strong it could not be defeated by more magic, but might feed off it and grow stronger. The force would be vanquished, I determined, only through courage, cleverness, imagination, good judgment, and good sense. I waited for someone with those qualities, for you. And you proved me right."

Grayling looked at him in wonder.

"I do have some useful skills," Sylvanus told her. "The school at Nether Finchbeck does not employ me merely for my handsome face. Now I must go."

He dropped a handful of copper coins into Grayling's hand. "Fare thee well, lass. Perchance we might meet again." He touched his hand to his head in a salute as he walked off, leading the mule one way, leaving Grayling and Auld Nancy and Pansy to go another.

Grayling called to Sylvanus, "You never told us — what is the *first* rule of magic?"

He spun round and called back to her, "'Tis the hardest rule to learn: magic is not the answer. Magic may be convenient, brilliant, even dazzling, but it is not the answer." He waved once to her before he turned and walked on.

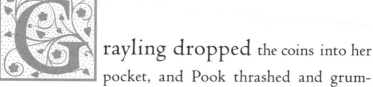rayling dropped the coins into her pocket, and Pook thrashed and grumbled in irritation as they landed on his head. Eager to see what awaited her, she turned her feet toward home. Where the road was rocky, she trod carefully, for the soles of her shoes were as thin as a poor man's soup. On paths smooth and soft she hurried her steps, though she felt ever so weary.

Auld Nancy, grown fine and thin and feeble, struggled, her shoulders slumped and breath ragged, and a sullen Pansy lagged behind. Pook slept most of the time in Grayling's pocket, snoring small mouse snores. Their adventures had tired him, too.

Days dragged on, but soon the world around her began to look familiar, and her heart leaped. She had admired that church, fancied that cottage, run from those dogs. It seemed a lifetime since they had passed this way. She had expected to be joyful and relieved after the defeat of the smoke and shadow, but her mind was uneasy, and her humors disordered. Her steps grew slower and slower as they passed the remnants of the silk pavilion, flapping in the autumn breeze.

They were near to the crossroads where the metal-nosed warlord had accosted them, and though travelers were plentiful on this stretch of road, Grayling's belly tightened with dread. To calm herself, she imagined the difficulties the man must have: sneezing his nose off, blowing a nose rusted in the rain, kissing Lady Metal Nose. She tried to laugh at the ridiculous images, but even as a daydream, his face frightened her, so she thought of more pleasant things: misty mornings, the smell of mint leaves brewed in hot water, robins in the spring, cabbage cooked with apples, yellow cheese and sausages and warm dark bread.

She turned to share this with Auld Nancy, but Auld

Nancy was a ways behind, sitting on the roadside with Pansy beside her.

"Turnips and thunderstorms," Grayling muttered in annoyance as she retraced her steps.

"Leave me, girl," said Auld Nancy. "I am weary in my bones and can go no farther."

"Fie, you know I would not leave you here," Grayling said. "Sit and rest those weary bones awhile, and I will join you, for if my feet could talk, they would whine and complain and beg for a rest." She dropped down beside the old woman.

Pansy's belly rumbled a loud rumble. "My belly is empty all the way to the ground," she said, "and these legs can go no more. There be an inn up this road. I saw it when we passed in the wagon of the warlord. Can we not spend some of Sylvanus's coins on bread and mayhap a bed?"

Grayling shook her head. "Nay, we may yet need them."

Pansy crossed her arms. "You sound like my mother. I have no need of another mother. I need supper."

Dark clouds moved over them and rain began, whispering through the trees and pocking the ground. Water dripping from her hair, her nose, her fingertips, Grayling turned to Auld Nancy. "Auld Nancy, we are discomfited enough. Will you not stop the rain?"

Auld Nancy shook her head as she lifted her bedraggled broom. "We no longer have the power, my broom and I."

Showers turned to downpour. Auld Nancy sneezed, and Grayling said, "Oh, drips and drizzles, it's the inn for us."

The three were soggy and chilled when they reached the inn on the outskirts of the town. Inside, it smelled like wet clothes, stale ale, and—Grayling sniffed— mutton stew, fragrant with garlic and pepper.

Auld Nancy dropped onto a bench at a table near the fire, while Grayling bargained with the innkeeper, a large young man with missing teeth in his broad smile. Returning to the others, Grayling said, "I have secured us bread, beer, and stew. There are no beds to be had, but we are welcome to sleep here by the fire."

Auld Nancy brightened a little. But where was Pansy? In the dim light of the inn, Grayling saw the girl speaking with two men near the door. "Pansy," Grayling called, "you complained of hunger, and I can hear your belly rumbling from here. Come and have supper."

Grayling found that her weariness made even a wooden bench comfortable enough for sleeping. Rain pelted the roof and the wind wailed as she closed her eyes, and it was near dawn when she woke. The inn- keeper was feeding great logs to the fire, and he winked at Grayling. "I shall warm some ale for ye, for 'tis a nasty morning indeed out there."

Grayling nodded her thanks and left the inn to relieve herself. Her hair tangled and her cloak whipped about her as she trudged from the inn and back, curs- ing the wind. But this wind did not blight her spirits or extinguish her will. Certes, then, it was mere wind. Wasn't it?

Pansy and Auld Nancy were stirring when she returned. "The rain has stopped," she told them, "although the wind is fierce. We shall not have easy walking today."

"No matter," said Pansy, looking pleased with her- self. "I sent word last night to the man with the metal nose, Lord Mandrake he is called, that the witches he sought before are here."

Grayling lurched forward and grabbed Pansy's arm. "What? Pansy, what have you done?"

Pansy shook off Grayling's hold. "I want to do magic, and if Sylvanus will not teach me, I will go to Lord Mandrake."

Grayling shook her head. "Pansy, he will cage you as he did before."

"I will gladly trade my freedom for power. With practice, my magic will grow stronger, and folks will cease their *poor Pansy*s and *foolish Pansy*s and be in awe of me!"

"He cannot be trusted."

"Nor can I. We will make a fine pair."

"But you have ensnarled *us*! Think on it. I have no magic, and Auld Nancy has exhausted hers. What will happen when your Lord Mandrake finds that out?"

Pansy shrugged. "You will think of something. Sylvanus says you have courage and keen wits." Her voice was sharp edged, and her eyes hard.

Grayling had endured Pansy long enough. Let her go where she willed, as long as it was far from Grayling. "We must be away without delay, Auld Nancy." Grayling helped her to her feet. "Before the warlord comes."

In a voice ragged and weary, Auld Nancy said, "Pansy, you have learned nothing from this misadventure, but are even more foolish and wicked. Do what you will." She took Grayling's arm, and they moved toward the door.

"Go, then," said Pansy. "I will be a powerful magician, rich beyond your dreams, and you will come to wish you had stayed. And been kinder to me!"

Grayling and Auld Nancy pushed the door open and stumbled out. The day was cold and sunless, and the air smelled of snow. The wind wolf-howled, and the tall firs swayed like grasses. Broken branches littered the road so that Grayling and Auld Nancy had to leap and skitter to stay afoot. *Fir cones and fiddlesticks, 'tis past time to be home,* Grayling thought as she pushed Auld Nancy faster and faster until darkness fell once more.

n the morning, Grayling found frost on her nose and her eyelashes. The air was filled with the noisy honking of geese, and she studied them as they passed overhead. How easily they moved and how much faster than human folks on foot. Grayling recalled persuading Pook the raven to stay on the ground where it was safer. Watching the geese, their undersides flashing white and gray, Grayling thought she might have been mistaken. How would the world look from up there? What could she see from the sky that she had never seen? Were she a bird, would she choose

to stay on the ground or soar, no matter the danger? She knew what she once would have said, but now she was not so certain.

The memory of Pook the raven moved her to take the mouse from her pocket and jiggle him awake. He opened his eyes and snuffled, with bits of acorn still adorning his whiskers. "Mistress Gray Eyes, do you wish the assistance of . . . " He yawned a great yawn — that is, great for a tiny creature like a mouse. ". . . this Pook?"

Grayling stroked his head gently. "I have been thinking 'tis a long while since you shifted into another shape."

Pook said in a faint, thin voice, "This mouse will likely not be taken with that again. I believe this Pook is only a mouse now."

"But a very special mouse," Grayling whispered. He coughed a tiny cough. "Are you quite well?"

"Aye," he said, "but weary. Most weary," and he slipped back into her pocket.

A late autumn market provided biscuits and pears and soft sweet cheese in exchange for the last of Sylvanus's coppers. Bellies full, they walked on, slower and slower as the morning grew later.

The cold sun was high in the sky when they neared the spot where they were to part ways.

"We must each set out for home now, Auld Nancy, or we shall freeze into statues here on the road." Grayling wrapped her cloak more tightly around her. "'Tis still a goodly walk for us both."

Auld Nancy dropped to the ground, broom in her lap.

Grayling gasped. "Auld Nancy, are you ill?"

"The fingers of giants are making shadows in the sky," Auld Nancy said.

Grayling looked up. "What mean you? I see only bare branches against the gray."

"Of course, tree branches." Auld Nancy shook her head. "It appears my bones and my wits are both failing me."

As she helped Auld Nancy struggle to her feet, Grayling felt her heart near pulled in two. She was most eager to be home, but she could not leave Auld Nancy to travel alone. With a sigh that she pulled all the way from her toes, Grayling said, "Come, we have walked all this way together. I will not leave you now. I shall see you home."

She tried to remember if her mother had a staying-alive song. Such a song was called for now, but if Hannah

Strong did, Grayling did not know it. Their footsteps beat out a sort of a tune, and words came into her head, and tune and words came together in a melody. With the old woman leaning heavily on her, Grayling began to walk, singing the song she was inventing as they went:

> Be strong, look around you,
> Blue asters are blooming, the yarrow is tall.
> Apples and sweet pears are yet on the tree.
> The wide world calls.
> Take my hand, take my hand.
>
> Winter will come soon.
> Your nose and your cheeks will pink with the cold
> When frost paints the walls
> And footsteps sing crunch songs
> To snowdrops and crocus.
>
> In spring you'll be walking
> In fields newly white-capped
> With marguerite daisies,
> As geese winging home honk their calls.
>
> Summer will sizzle and warm your old bones,
> As you lie in the meadow and look forward to fall.
> Stay alive, Auld Nancy, for living is all,
> Full of promise and friendship.
> Take my hand, take my hand.

"Hannah Strong is indeed a fine one for making songs," said Auld Nancy. "I vow, I feel stronger."

"I most sincerely hope so," said Grayling, "but that is my own song that I just now made and none of my mother's."

"So you have her song skill as well as her wisdom and her strength."

Grayling nodded. *I do. It seems I do.*

They climbed up and down, through woods chilly and damp, rich with the smell of mushrooms and decaying wood. In places Grayling saw small trees standing on their roots as if on tiptoe. Auld Nancy followed her gaze. "The nurse logs have rotted away," she said. "The young trees need them no longer and grow on their own."

On their own. Grayling nodded in understanding.

The day wore on, and finally they saw the smoke from many hearth fires. There backed against a hill was a village. Auld Nancy sighed, and her face grew calm. "My heart is lifting now I am near to my bed," she said. She directed Grayling to turn here and there and no, not that path, this path.

They kept to the edge of the village. Those passing by bowed their heads to Auld Nancy, but Grayling could smell an uneasy stew of fear and awe and need. The very trees whispered *weather witch, weather witch.*

At the far end of the village was a stone hut with an arched wooden door painted green. Inside, the hut was drafty, cold, and damp, but bearable once Grayling found the tinderbox and started a fire. Smoke found its way around the room and out the smoke hole in the roof.

"Smoke yet frightens me," Grayling said to Auld Nancy.

"Only the foolish have no fear. There is much in this world to be fearful of, but much to bring pleasure if we have our wits about us." Auld Nancy groaned as she lay down on a thin pallet near the fire, which Grayling fed with twigs and seed cones dry enough to burn. She turned out the remains of the biscuits and cheese, and Auld Nancy directed her to a crock of cider and two mugs.

Grayling joined Auld Nancy on her pallet, and they supped.

Auld Nancy reached out and gently touched the scar that remained on Grayling's cheek. "You bear here a remembrance of our journey," she said.

"Auld Nancy," Grayling asked, "tell me truly: do

you think 'tis over? That the wise folk are themselves again and not rooted to the ground, now that the force is vanquished? And will all be well, though Pansy has gone to the warlord with her hurtful magic?"

"I do not know, but I have hope. Hope is an excellent and necessary thing to have in this world. Hope and bread and good friends." She sighed in satisfaction. "Now I am home, girl, and my belly full, I think I just might live."

"Indeed I think you might, and ere long, you will have your weather magic back and be again cloud pusher, fog mistress, she who controls the rain." Grayling paused a moment to frame a question and then asked, "What does magic feel like?"

Auld Nancy stared into the distance. "Using magic is like flying a kite. You think you are in control of it but then the wind catches it — it tugs and then shoots away like an arrow released from a bow."

As it had done for Pansy, Grayling thought. "Sylvanus says true magic is like a sausage, made of bits and pieces of things we all have."

"Aye, true. Magic be a paradox, everything and nothing," said Auld Nancy.

"Pansy has skill and real power. Not everyone has such. I do not."

"Pansy's is a powerful, greedy, wicked sort of magic. You too have skills." Auld Nancy yawned and stretched. "But even better, you have good sense and a caring heart, sharp eyes in your head, and the wits to use them. No matter what magic she has or learns, Pansy will never have that."

Grayling nodded. It was enough.

Pook climbed slowly out of Grayling's pocket and scoured the floor for crumbs and seeds. With a squeak of contentment, he climbed onto the pallet and settled down next to her to groom his whiskers.

The next morning, Grayling prepared to begin her walk home. She wrapped Desdemona Cork's shawl around Auld Nancy's frail shoulders and tied it tight. "I am reluctant to bid farewell to you, for I have grown fond of you and your grumbles."

Auld Nancy smiled and said, "And I, you. You have cared for me most tenderly." She took two wrinkled apples from a green bowl, wrapped the last biscuits and large crumbs of the remaining cheese in a cloth, and gave the bundle to Grayling for her journey. Grayling gave the old woman a quick hug.

"Pook," she said to the mouse, who was cleaning his paws with a tiny pink tongue, "we must be off.

'Tis a long walk to my valley." Her heart gave a little flutter.

With a squeak and a sigh, the mouse said, "Mistress, this mouse is wearied from the traveling and quite elderly for a mouse." He coughed once and continued in a weaker voice. "This mouse would stay here."

Grayling was surprised at the rush of sadness and loss she felt. "Are you certain? What shall I do without you?"

"Ahh, Gray Eyes . . ." His voice grew faint and feathery, and he shuddered.

Her eyes burned. How could she leave him behind? They had been through so much, and she loved him. A mouse, and she loved him. She swallowed hard and said, "Then farewell, Pook. You are a prince of a mouse, a wonder of a mouse, an entirely splendid mouse, and I shall miss you." *Terribly,* she thought with a snuffle.

Pook had turned aside for a fit of cleaning and paid no attention to her, continuing to groom his paws. He looked different . . . quite mouselike. Grayling bit her lip and looked away. This mouse was a mouse now and Pook no longer.

She wrapped her cloak about her, took her bundle, and set off alone into the morning mist.

XVII

he road ran ever on, through hills and fields, meadows and valleys, past towns and villages. After two weary days and frosty nights, Grayling woke with empty belly but full heart. Today she would be home.

The sun was rising as she climbed up the hill she had once walked down. Here and there she could hear the jabbering song of a starling, although bare-branched oaks, alders, and maples warned, "Autumn is waning. Make ready for winter." She made a song to sing along:

Seasons change, winter's nigh.
Leaves change color, fall, and die.
Seasons change, wet and dry.
Even wise folk wonder why
Everything changes by and by.

Humming, she reached the rise where she had slept that first night and thought once more of Pook, safe and warm and well fed with Auld Nancy. Grayling patted the pocket where she had carried him to the sea and back. "Never," she whispered, as though he could hear her, "never did I think I would miss having a mouse in my pocket. Or a goat by my side. But I do."

Still, down from this hill was her mother—her mother whole and out of danger, she hoped, or her mother growing into the ground, or her mother a tree now, but still her mother. Grayling's heart thumped in anticipation as she headed into the valley.

She peered through the trees, trying to catch sight of the cottage or at least what part of it survived the fire. Faint remains of the smoke scented the air, and Grayling imagined the ruins would be like broken teeth upon the ground. But as she grew nigh, she felt dizzy with joy and relief. There was the cottage, much as it had been—small, to be sure, but solid and sturdy, roofed with freshly laid thatch. The walls were repaired with oak timbers and patched with woven-stick wattle under daub of mud, dung, and straw.

And there was her mother—no roots, no branches, no leaves—her mother, Hannah Strong! Grayling smiled so wide it hurt her face, and she half stumbled, half danced down the path, her hair flying and her cheeks burning. "Hannah Strong!" she shouted. "Mother, I am home!"

The woman turned. Her daub-spattered kirtle hung loosely, and the hair peeping out from beneath her kerchief was gray. Had her mother changed so much in this past fortnight, or had Grayling not noticed her aging? But grizzled or not, the woman was not a tree, and her legs ended not in roots but in wide, strong feet.

"Well met, daughter," said Hannah Strong, thrusting a handful of sticky daub at Grayling. "Take some of this and help me. I wish to have solid walls before the snows come."

Grayling put her hands out without thinking and accepted the heavy, soggy heap.

"Where is the grimoire?" asked Hannah Strong.

"'Tis part of my story. Shall I tell it? Do you wish to know what I found and what I did and how it is you are no longer rooted to the ground?"

Hannah Strong waved her muddy hand. "Pish. There are mysteries aplenty in this world, and I have not the time to question them all."

"But it was my doing, and—"

Hannah Strong pushed Grayling toward the cottage wall. "Tell me when daylight has faded. Go and be useful."

Now she was home and faced with Hannah Strong, Grayling felt childish and insignificant again, as if the past weeks had not happened at all. But they had, and she had much to tell. "I expect my story can keep," she said as she spread the daub upon the wall, "but do say how the cottage has been made whole again. It can be only a short time since the spell was broken and you were freed."

"The Tailor twins wanted my remedy for wind in the bowels, and the price was repair to the cottage frame. Goodwife Stock needed a love potion, so she helped me weave the wattle. And you can see what Thomas Thatcher paid for relief for his griping gut," said Hannah Strong, gesturing toward the roof. She slapped another handful of daub on the side of the cottage and spread it thickly. "We must finish the plastering soon, for there are salves and potions to be mixed, brewed, and bottled."

Grayling stopped, daub dripping from her hands down her skirt. "Indeed. Your salves and potions were lost or gone with me. What, then, did you give to Goodwife Stock and the others?"

"I made do," said Hannah Strong. "I had herbs and spells and fresh water, ashes and berries and songs. And I am quite adept at persuasion."

Grayling smiled. Her mother's magic was indeed like a sausage.

Day darkened to chilly evening as they daubed the cottage walls.

Finally they cleaned their hands and took shelter in the unfinished cottage. The room was smaller than Grayling remembered, empty and cold and lacking the chairs and tables and shelves of supplies that had made it home.

She built a small fire with bits of charred wood and tinder and warmed her backside. Hannah Strong unwrapped a parcel of cheese and brown bread and a jug of sour ale. Grayling raised an eyebrow in query. "Simon Strand the innkeeper," said Hannah Strong, "wished a tonic to sweeten his mother-in-law's disposition."

Grayling sat and nestled close to the hearth.

"Tell me now," Hannah Strong said as they ate.

So Grayling began with the mouse who ate the potions and singing in the towns and the woman with the wart. "And can you guess," she asked, "who heard me singing and came to me?"

But her mother was asleep.

It rained that night, but the roof was tight and the walls nearly so, so Grayling was dry and almost warm. She thought of Auld Nancy, who could stop this rain — if she wished, if she was rested and her belly was full. Grayling was struck with a sudden yearning to see her, which she held close until she, too, slept.

She dreamed of hissing serpents and woke with a start, but the sound proved only the hissing of the damp wood in the fire. She was home. She turned with a huff and slept again, dreamless.

In the morning, as they finished the remains of the cheese, Hannah Strong said, "The brown clay pot there is some cracked from the heat of the fire but likely will serve. Go and gather bilberries and thistle, bayberry bark and the roots of what yellow dock is still in the garden, and we will brew healing tonics. Certes there will soon be problems that cannot be eased with chanting, mint, and persuasion." She added more wood to the fire and blew it into greater flame.

Grayling wrapped her cloak around her, took the brown clay pot, and went outside. The rain had stopped. She searched through the shriveled herbs outside for what was yet alive and useful. Then she sat, resting her weary body and her blistered feet, and fell asleep there in the garden. That day and the next passed, filled with some labor, a bit of food, and welcome sleep.

Grayling felt strangely restless and dissatisfied. Something was missing, something Grayling needed to feel safe and content as she used to. The valley she had longed for seemed somehow empty and forlorn. What was happening in the world outside? Was the metal-nosed warlord still brewing disorder? Was Pansy trying out more selfish magic?

The third morning, she woke early and left the cottage, weary of the smell of charred wood and fresh daub.

It was too cold for bird song, but she heard water gurgling through the small round rocks in the pond, and she began humming along.

For a moment she imagined she heard the grimoire singing, and she stopped cold. For many days, she had sung to it and heard it sing back, but lately she and the grimoire had been silent. She missed the song, the tug and the promise, the satisfaction of having something important to do. And others to do it with.

Taking a deep breath and hoping, Grayling began to sing. And as faint as the whoosh of a butterfly's wings, she heard the grimoire's song. Wherever Phinaeus Moon and the book were, no water lay between them and Grayling. She sang again for the pleasure of hearing the grimoire, sea-soaked and far away, sing back.

While Hannah Strong smoothed another coat of daub on the cottage walls, Grayling searched for what was available and edible. She gathered rosehips and ripe plums and dug for wild garlic. There were withered pears on a tree and shriveled blackberries. Once inside, Hannah Strong brought out the heel of bread. Such a supper reminded Grayling of meals on the road, and she remembered the lovely Desdemona Cork with the sun and moon inked on her face. What did she do now? And

Auld Nancy, Sylvanus, and Phinaeus Moon? Did they think of her and sigh, as she did?

The music of raindrops on the cottage roof moved Grayling to make a song, but instead she fell into a tired sleep. That night she dreamed of flying goats and singing cheese and men with horses' feet.

Next morning Grayling sought her mother, who was out gathering sticks and twigs for the fire. "Sit, Mother," Grayling said, and her voice trembled. "You must listen. I have things to say, and it is time to say them." She cleared her throat and began again. "Stop working, sit, and listen. I have seen much and lived much since I left you, and I was changed by my adventures." She smiled with the remembering. "My story has a serpent, magicians, and soothsaying cheeses. I was brave at times, and I discovered many things I can do and know."

Without protest, Hannah Strong wiped her hands clean on her kirtle and sat down on the firewood stack to listen. As Grayling told her story, she wondered again that she had had the courage to leave her home and face such dangers.

Hannah Strong nodded her head while Grayling spoke. "Aye," she said when Grayling finished. "I have heard whispers and rumors that other cunning folk were rooted as I was and now have been freed, grimoires taken and now returned. And that was your doing?"

"I considered what I must do to free you, and I did it. I expect you are surprised to hear that."

"Not a bit," said Hannah Strong. "I never would have sent you if I had not known you could do it."

"Truly?" Grayling felt her cheeks grow warm with pleasure and surprise. "You never told me that."

"I did not think it needed telling. You did what must be done."

"I did! I did!" But even as she said it, Grayling realized it was not true. *They* had done it, all of them together.

She pulled at a loose thread on her tattered skirt. Just as one thread is not as strong as woven cloth, she thought, a person striving with others can be stronger than she would be alone. She had never thought of that before. She was swept with longing for the others.

Hannah Strong slapped her knee and rose. "Enough. It was a good journey and a good story, and now we must hurry and make ready for winter. When rain and snow fall, I would have us be safe and content within." She studied Grayling and said, "Wise women learn when they are ready, and I believe your journey has made you ready.

I will share my spells with you and teach you more of my songs — everything the wise woman's daughter needs to know."

A soft breeze blew into the valley. It reminded Grayling of the sea breeze, and she took a fine deep breath. The world seemed to grow wider, in ripples, as if she, Grayling, were a pebble thrust into a pond, and the whole world swirled in circles around her. She knew not what would come of it but felt such a yearning that she could not withstand it. Tucking a sprig of bright red holly berries in her hair, she smiled.

Grayling hurried back into the cottage for her cloak and out again. She found a stout walking stick and looked up the hill she had so recently come down.

Hannah Strong's shoulders sagged as she watched the girl. "I knew from the moment I sent you to save me that this day would come, but so soon?"

"I cannot stay. I trust you can find others to help you boil and brew and learn your songs. I may be the wise woman's daughter, but I have my own song to sing." Grayling put her arms around her mother. "I will fetch your grimoire from Phinaeus Moon and see it returned to you."

"Nay, girl, I believe 'tis yours now. From mother to

daughter, over generations." Her mother, not one for hugging, yet hugged Grayling back.

"Farewell, Hannah Strong," Grayling said.

"Farewell, daughter."

In her clear true voice, Grayling sang her new song:

> *Seasons change, winter's nigh.*
> *Leaves change color, fall, and die.*
> *Seasons change, wet and dry.*
> *Even wise folk wonder why*
> *Everything changes by and by.*

She stopped for a moment and then nodded and added a last line:

> *Seasons change, and so do I.*

Then Grayling turned for the path back up the hill toward the rest of the world.

AUTHOR'S NOTE

Cunning folk? Wise women? Hedge witches? I knew there was a story there, and the only way I could find out what it was was to write it. So I did, setting the story in a place much like medieval England but with magic.

For centuries, all across the world, cunning folk, also called wise women or wise men or hedge witches, were the ones villagers sought out to cure toothache or bellyache, to find lost or stolen objects, or to provide love potions and prophecies. The activities of cunning folk could be sorted into herbal medicine, folk magic, and divination. Some of their pursuits may sound far-fetched to modern ears, but they were recognized remedies in medieval England, and much of what cunning folk found and did is still used today.

HERBAL MEDICINE

The use of plants as medicines dates as far back as the origin of humankind. Historic sites in Iraq show that Neanderthals used yarrow, marsh-mallow root, and other herbs more than sixty thousand years ago.

People have always relied on plants for nourishment. Through trial and error, they discovered that some plants are good to eat, some are poisonous, and some produce bodily changes or relieve pain. Over time, these observations were passed down from generation to generation, with each new population adding to the body of knowledge.

Many ancient plant-based remedies are used to this day, such as ginger and mint to treat nausea, poppies to make medicine for sedation and pain relief, and witch hazel lotion for skin ailments. Saint John's wort, once used to ward off evil spirits, now relieves depression. Spiderwebs have been used since Roman times on wounds to stop the bleeding. It is now known that spiderwebs are rich in vitamin K, which can be effective in clotting blood. Even carnivorous animals are known to consume plants when ill. My cat eats grass.

Valuable modern medicines are derived from herbal folk

remedies: from the moldy bread used on wounds to speed healing came penicillin; from willow bark, used for fevers, came aspirin; foxglove, used to treat various complaints, led to digitoxin for heart trouble.

In March 2015, scientists at the University of Nottingham in England reported that they had tried a thousand-year-old Anglo-Saxon remedy for sties, or infections of the eyelids: *Take crop leek and garlic, of both equal quantities, pound them well together . . . Take wine and bullocks gall* [bile from the gall bladder of a steer], *mix with the leek . . . Let it stand nine days in the brass vessel.* The bizarre-sounding potion was then tested on skin taken from mice infected with the antibiotic-resistant superbug MRSA. It killed 90 percent of the bacteria! And the Anglo-Saxons knew about it more than a thousand years ago.

Not all ancient remedies were actually helpful, however, and some sound loathsome — fried mouse for whooping cough, for example, or boiled sheep droppings for smallpox, or boiled onions carried in the armpits to cure pneumonia.

FOLK MAGIC

Herbal healing, like life in general long ago, was mixed with magic and superstition. Charms or amulets, objects believed to have magical powers (like a rabbit's foot), were carried to ward off illness or misfortune. Specific actions or gestures, such as hand motions against the evil eye, were assumed to have magical powers. Think of Auld Nancy waving her broom at a rainy sky.

Spells, chants, and incantations are magical words or phrases intended to bring about a specific result. "Hocus-pocus" and "abracadabra" are magic words used by many magicians. The Amazing Mumford on *Sesame Street* used "A la peanut butter sandwiches!"; Ali Baba in the Arabian *Nights* called out "Open Sesame!" and the door opened. Auld Nancy, Pansy, and Sylvanus all use spells or chants, with varying results. Grayling's song to the grimoire is a magical incantation.

DIVINATION

Used in various cultures throughout history, both ancient and modern, divination is the practice of seeking knowledge of the future or the unknown by reading signs or omens. In contemporary society, it is encountered in the form of astrology, tarot cards, the *I Ching*, and the Ouija board. Reading tea leaves or the lines on one's palm are other types of divination.

For more than five thousand years, diviners, such as Sylvanus, have read prophecies in all manner of objects, including dust (abacomancy), spiders (arachnomancy), entrails of animals (haruspicy), the howling of dogs (ololygmancy), and, of course, cheese (tyromancy). Their prophecies were taken seriously and probably changed the course of history more than once. Today, although few read the future in animal entrails, millions of people practice a form of divination by consulting their daily horoscope or flipping a coin to make a decision.